As Josh's arms closed around her, Diane had the sense of poising on a threshold

Beyond lay the danger of a broken heart and a boatload of regret. But she longed for Josh with a razor-edge of desire and a rush of tenderness. "No promises," she warned.

"I can handle that." Catching her waist, he ran his thumbs lightly up her rib cage.

As hunger filled her, she touched his face and then, emboldened, kissed the pulse of his neck. As if he belonged to her. As if she had the right to touch him whenever she pleased.

And for today, she did.

"Let's take this indoors," he murmured.

Once through the door, Josh whirled her across the living room. She lost her flip-flops en route. Barefoot and wild—totally unlike her usual self.

About to get a lot wilder.

Dear Reader,

HARMONY CIRCLE is set in the real town of Brea, California. I loved developing the interconnected characters in this book, the first of a trilogy. As you'll see, they meet new friends, encounter old acquaintances, gossip, argue and, most rewarding of all, find love.

The idea of Josh serving as a holdout juror arose when, while preparing to write this book, I served on a jury. We heard a civil suit over a traffic collision, not a murder case, but I found the process inherently dramatic. As so often happens with authors, the experience gave me an idea.

In two further books we'll follow the other characters you meet here, along with new ones. I hope you enjoy them!

Best,

Jacqueline Diamond

The Family Next Door

JACQUELINE DIAMOND

HARLEQUIN®

TORONTO • NEW YORK • LONDON
AMSTERDAM • PARIS • SYDNEY • HAMBURG
STOCKHOLM • ATHENS • TOKYO • MILAN • MADRID
PRAGUE • WARSAW • BUDAPEST • AUCKLAND

ISBN-13: 978-0-373-75213-3
ISBN-10:   0-373-75213-X

THE FAMILY NEXT DOOR

www.eHarlequin.com

Printed in U.S.A.

ABOUT THE AUTHOR

Jacqueline Diamond lives in a Southern California community a lot like Harmony Circle, where people fall in love, fall out of love, serve on juries, plant and cut down trees, and survive their children's teenage years. She invites readers to check out her Web site, www.jacquelinediamond.com, for her latest news, and e-mail her at jdiamondfriends@yahoo.com.

Books by Jacqueline Diamond

HARLEQUIN AMERICAN ROMANCE

*Downhome Doctors

To Elizabeth Rudd, who is truly a great teacher

Chapter One

Removing the old playhouse from the slope behind Diane Bittner's house had been on her to-do list for ages. But she'd put it off because the ginger cat that hung out in her yard liked to sun itself on the roof. Also because her late husband, Will, had put a lot of love into planning and overseeing the construction. Whenever she looked at it, she saw him once again, grinning at their daughter's eagerness to stage her first tea party.

Now, at twelve, Brittany had outgrown the playhouse, which was succumbing to dry rot. Eventually, Diane planned to hire someone to remove it, but September had arrived already and she was busy with her fourth-grade class.

Perhaps she should have been grateful then, when one Saturday afternoon the new neighbor behind her—the man whose hammering and sawing had been making her life miserable for weeks—dropped a tree on it.

But she wasn't.

First, the crash scared the stuffing out of the cat, Lucy, who leaped off her perch just seconds before the pine slammed down. With a screech of protest, Lucy sailed through the air, hit the ground running and disappeared.

Second, the crash startled Brittany into jerking a spatula out of the cake batter she was mixing. Yellow goo fanned across the kitchen table, nearly splattering Diane, who sat writing welcome notes to her students.

"What was *that?*" Her daughter stared through the kitchen window toward the slope. "Mom, there's a tree on my playhouse!"

Diane sat frozen, as her heart thundered inside her chest. The crash had yanked her backward two years to another boom that had erupted out of nowhere. One minute she and Will had been strolling happily through a street fair, and the next, he was crumpled on the pavement, with a bullet in his chest. Diane's childhood sweetheart and husband of nearly a dozen years had died as paramedics struggled to save him.

"Mom!" Her daughter's voice pulled her back to the present.

Shaking off her anxiety, Diane got to her feet and peered out the window. The playhouse lay crushed beneath a large tree that had tumbled over the iron fence separating her yard from the one behind.

This new neighbor was dangerously careless, Diane fumed. Why on earth had he sawed into a tree without calculating where it would land?

Noisy renovations had begun almost immediately after the man's arrival. The fellow—a divorcé with a daughter, according to Diane's neighbors in the Harmony Circle development—hadn't bothered to stop by and introduce himself, let alone apologize for the racket. People were usually more considerate in Brea, a smallish town tucked into a cozy inland corner of Orange County, California.

That must be her neighbor now, opening the gate in the fence. At last he was going to have to apologize.

As he descended the stone steps embedded on one side of

the sloping perimeter, Diane reluctantly noticed the easy sway of his jeans-clad hips and the muscular expanse of his chest. The breeze ruffled the man's dark-blond hair as he surveyed the damage.

"Gee, he's kind of cute," Brittany declared. "I mean, for an older guy."

There was something familiar about him. Something that, despite his good looks, made Diane uneasy. "What's he doing?" she groused.

"I think he's looking inside, to see if anybody got hurt." Brittany started for the back door. "Aren't you coming?"

"Of course." Diane decided she could hardly blame a man for fixing up his property—and mistakes did happen. While these weren't the best circumstances for a first encounter, at least he'd apparently come to set things right.

On the bright side, he'd no doubt offer to remove what was left of the structure, which would save Diane the expense. Private-school teachers didn't earn a lot, and her finances had been on a tight leash ever since her husband's death.

After mopping up the cake batter, she followed her daughter through the den and out the sliding glass door to the patio. Shading her gaze against the sun, Diane heard the man calling, "Hello? Anybody hurt?"

She appreciated his concern. And once again she couldn't help noticing his easy, muscular movements.

Not that she took any personal interest. Her mother and sister, who lived across the street, kept urging Diane to date. But she was nowhere near ready to seek a replacement for the gentle man who'd been her soul mate.

Then the stranger straightened and faced her. When he met her gaze, she received her second shock of the afternoon.

She knew him.

His name was Josh Lawrence or Lorenzo or something like that. Better known as Juror Number Seven at the trial of the gunman who'd shot her husband.

A minority of one on an otherwise sensible jury, he'd allowed the killer to go free.

JOSH LORENZ couldn't believe the new gardener he'd hired had made such a boneheaded miscalculation. His intention to supervise the work had been interrupted by a phone call that had sent him inside to consult a file on his computer and it had all happened so fast.

Josh took pride in hiring only the most skilled professionals, whether for himself or for the clients he served as a building contractor. Now he'd sent this new guy packing before racing over to apologize and to make amends.

Until today, he'd avoided his neighbor. Too bad the real estate agent hadn't mentioned her name until after escrow closed. Even though he'd have hated to lose the place, Josh had no desire to inflict any further pain on Diane Bittner.

Across the backyard, the rear slider scraped open and a girl about his daughter's age emerged. That must be Diane's daughter, Brittany.

Behind her, he glimpsed a woman with long golden-brown hair, whose dark eyes were rapidly widening with alarm. A hum of response swept through Josh. He felt as if he knew her intimately as a result of those weeks in the courtroom and her testimony on the witness stand.

His final sight of her had come after the judge had dismissed the hopelessly hung jury. As she stood in a corridor of the Orange County Superior Courthouse surrounded by the eleven jurors who disagreed with him, Josh had slipped by, certain that he'd done his conscientious best.

All the same, he wished he hadn't been the one to bring further distress into her life.

Since then, the scenario had often replayed itself in his mind. Hector Fry, a nineteen-year-old ex-gang member, claimed he'd fired out a window by accident while snatching away his mother's loaded gun from a five-year-old relative. The prosecution, seeking a conviction for second-degree murder, contended that Hector had remained loyal to his gang and was aiming at rival gang members attending a street fair.

Based on court testimony and documents admitted into evidence, Josh had formed a reasonable doubt about the young man's guilt. It had seemed so at the time, anyway, although the anguish evident on Diane Bittner's gentle face when the foreman read the verdict haunted his dreams for months afterward.

Well, that was water under the bridge. Or a smashed playhouse under a pine tree, in this case.

She reached the foot of the slope. Even on a warm Saturday, when most of the women in Brea would have tossed on shorts and a tank top, Diane Bittner had dressed in a crisp print blouse and tailored slacks. An elegant woman with a generous mouth and understated femininity, she made Josh keenly aware of his stained T-shirt and all the calluses he'd developed over the years of construction work.

"Mrs. Bittner," he said politely.

"Mr...um...Lawrence?" Tension strained her voice.

"Lorenz. First name's Josh." He considered extending a hand and then decided against it. For one thing, the lady might not welcome the gesture. For another, his hands were far from clean. "I'm really sorry about the mess. I'll fix the damage, of course."

Her daughter broke what threatened to become an awkward silence. "I'm Brittany." She smiled at Josh, all sweetness and innocence in a flowered apron that his daughter, Carly, wouldn't have worn for a million bucks. Josh's rebellious off-spring refused to put on anything that wasn't black or purple, although underneath that prickly exterior there remained a young girl who still had the power to melt his heart.

"Pleased to meet you." He was glad Will Bittner's only child hadn't attended the trial. Nobody deserved to lose a parent that way, or to hear the painful details dragged out in court.

"My mom's name is Diane," the young girl volunteered.

"I'm pleased to meet her, too." In truth, they hadn't met, despite sitting a dozen feet apart throughout the trial.

Diane pressed her lips together. Apparently, this meeting distressed her beyond words.

Josh felt bad all over again. But a little irked, as well. He'd done his best to be fair. Jurors were just ordinary people trying to sift through the evidence as best they could.

"We were going to tear down the playhouse anyway," Brittany told him. In her apron pocket, a cell phone rang. "Excuse me."

He couldn't remember the last time Carly had said, "Excuse me." Once when he'd reminded her of her manners, she'd joked, "What is this, Buckingham Palace?"

Okay, so his daughter was a smart aleck. She'd had plenty of sarcastic things to say about moving here from nearby La Habra and about the private school in which he'd enrolled her. But the move marked an important step toward Josh's goal of ensuring them both stability and self-sufficiency.

She'd be all right once she made some friends.

The two adults were standing there awkwardly when Brittany clicked off. "Mom, I forgot I promised to help Suzy with her math. She's home babysitting her brother. May I go?"

Carly would have muttered, "See ya," and whisked out the

door while Josh was pumping her for details. Still, she generally behaved well around other adults.

"Of course, honey," Diane said.

"My best friend lives down the block," Brittany explained. To her mother, she said, "I'll put the batter in the fridge. Don't try to bake the cake yourself, okay? I'm going to make layers with filling. And *please* don't use the butter for anything else. I need it all for the icing."

Josh hadn't realized girls this age ever ventured into a kitchen except to grab a snack. "That sounds delicious."

Brittany grinned. "I'll save you a piece. I love people who aren't on diets. Nice to meet you."

She kissed her mother on the cheek and departed. Diane's expression softened as she watched the girl sweep into the house.

When she returned her attention to him, a pucker formed between brows—as shapely as the rest of her. Although there was nothing blatant about this woman, her delicate features and air of restrained sensuality tantalized Josh.

His tastes, which had once run to glamour girls, must finally be maturing. Not that the change would do him any good. Diane Bittner probably rated him somewhat lower than pond scum.

Returning to the business at hand, he indicated the fallen tree. "I can cut that up for firewood." All the houses in this neighborhood came with fireplaces, regardless of southern California's famous good weather. "And remove the playhouse, if that suits you. What were you planning to replace it with? I'd be happy to grade the soil for you, too. Looks like the perfect spot for a gazebo."

Her gaze shifted to the damaged structure. "I hadn't thought about what I'd put there. Doesn't grading require special equipment?"

"No problem. I'm a building contractor." Josh patted his

pockets, finding keys but no business card. "I should write down my phone number. Also, I'll need yours." Seeing her hesitation, he added, "To check with you before I intrude on your property. I'm afraid I haven't brought any paper, though."

She frowned. "I'd rather not... Oh, never mind. We might as well be civil, since we *are* neighbors. But that's as far as it goes." Diane turned and walked back to the house, her honey-brown hair swinging with an easy rhythm.

Josh hurried after her, grateful for even a modest truce. At the sliding door, he stepped out of his battered loafers and entered, immediately responding to the soothing scent of vanilla.

Then his eyes came to rest on a large image of a beaming, tuxedo-clad William Bittner on his wedding day, one arm encircling his radiant bride. Among various informal shots surrounding it was one the prosecutor had displayed in the courtroom, of the new father gazing lovingly at a baby in his arms.

A good man. Certainly a much more solid member of society than the confused kid who'd shot him.

Josh pulled his eyes away to survey the adjacent kitchen. The cabinets showed wear, the linoleum needed replacing and the dishwasher, oven and stovetop were all at least fifteen years old. Yet the cheerful wallpaper and flowered curtains spoke of a real home in a way that no decorator model could match.

Diane wrote her phone number on a slip of paper and Josh followed suit. As they stood side by side, the top of her head just reached his jawline. He registered the appealing fragrance of rose-scented shampoo.

The overhead lighting flickered. "Those fluorescent tubes should be replaced," he observed.

"I just replaced them. It didn't help," she replied impatiently.

He understood her frustration. He had the same fixtures

in his house, at least until he got around to replacing them. "The ballast—the transformers—must be shot. I could take care of that."

She stiffened. "I'd rather hire someone. Thanks all the same."

Josh didn't see the point in paying top dollar for such a minor job. Besides, he enjoyed helping people. "Are you sure?"

"Frankly, I'd prefer that we have as little..." Diane took another glance outside and then stopped talking, open-mouthed.

It was a common reaction to his eleven-year-old daughter, Josh reflected as he spotted Carly. Apparently considering the unlatched gate to be an invitation, she was clumping down the stone steps with a camera slung over her shoulder.

She'd tied back her untidy pink-and-purple-streaked hair, leaving random bits sticking out. The hem of her black skirt dragged on the grass and there was a rip beneath the arm of her purple jersey. As a finishing touch, she was wearing a pair of granny boots.

Carly had purchased the outfit, along with most of her other clothes, at a thrift store in their former hometown, sniffing at Josh's offers to take her to the mall here in Brea. She'd also chosen bright-green braces for her teeth instead of the traditional silver, and her fingernails were painted a shade of purple so dark that it was almost black.

"That one's mine," he admitted. "She and Brittany must be about the same age."

"I expect so, since they're both in sixth grade."

Josh gave a start. He'd forgotten that Diane taught at Brea Academy, which accepted students from kindergarten through eighth grade. "She's in your class?"

"No. I teach fourth grade. But she does stand out. She's usually alone, even at lunch." Momentarily, Diane seemed to forget her dislike of him as she watched the girl photograph the ruined playhouse from several angles. He admired her for allowing her instincts as a teacher and mother come to the fore. "She always carries that camera. It puts a wall between her and other people, doesn't it?"

He'd never considered his child's hobby in that light. "That wasn't the idea when I bought it. Quite the opposite." Pleased when Carly had expressed interest in a hobby, he'd splurged on the camera last Christmas. To him, photography had seemed a means of engaging the world, not keeping it at bay.

"She's so isolated," Diane continued thoughtfully. "Any particular reason for that?"

Although she was prying, Josh didn't mind. He was glad she'd set her resentment aside. More importantly, on the subject of his daughter, he needed all the help he could get.

"Her mother left when she was seven, and her stepfather isn't crazy about kids," he explained. "Tiffany pops in and out of Carly's life when it suits her. That plays havoc with her emotions."

Diane nodded. "She should get to know Brittany and Suzy. She'll adjust more easily if she has friends outside school."

She'd allow his daughter to hang out with hers? That was quite a generous concession.

"I appreciate that. Brittany seems amazingly well-adjusted, considering…" Josh halted, mortified.

Diane's shoulders were absolutely rigid. Darn, did he always have to put his foot in his mouth? "She's very kind. And that was generous, offering me a slice of cake," he added quickly.

She avoided his gaze. "Please don't encourage her. She latches onto father figures much too easily. Her grandmother and aunt live across the street, but that doesn't seem to help all that much."

"I'm not sure I know how to discourage her," Josh admitted. "I'd hate to hurt her feelings."

"Well, figure out a way, or she'll be showering you with baked goods. I don't want to have to tell her who you... What you did."

The thought troubled Josh. "I'm truly sorry my position upset you, but I had a reasonable doubt. I still do."

"And I have reasonable doubt about your sanity." Anger flashed across Diane's face.

The pain of her loss was obviously still raw, even after two years. Josh appreciated what a terrific husband and father Will Bittner must have been. If he could restore the man to life, he'd do it. But sacrificing the confused, good-hearted kid who'd shot him wouldn't have accomplished that.

Outside, his daughter chose that uncomfortable moment to start toward the Bittners' house. Josh hoped she hadn't noticed them arguing. And wondered how he was going to explain it, if she had.

For his daughter's sake, he'd hate to see this issue come out in the open.

Chapter Two

Diane's heart had gone out to Carly Lorenz the first day of school as she'd watched the sixth-grader shooting pictures of her classmates instead of talking to them. Put off by her odd appearance and by the intrusiveness of the camera, her classmates gave her a wide berth.

To Diane, the girl's air of innocence belied the in-your-face attire and makeup, and she'd resolved to keep tabs on the situation. However, the needs of her own students came first, and so far she hadn't had a chance to get acquainted.

While loyalty to her husband's memory demanded that she have as little as possible to do with Josh Lorenz, she could hardly brush off his daughter. Besides, despite his infuriating refusal to admit he'd been wrong about Hector Fry, he'd behaved decently both about the fallen tree and her malfunctioning lights, which he'd offered to repair.

She hated to admit how much she could use the help. Good handymen were hard to find, and they didn't come cheap in Orange County.

Wait. No. She couldn't allow Josh regular access to her house. He was too…tempting. To Brittany, as a father substitute. Also, in all honesty, Diane found his unselfconscious masculinity disconcerting. She missed the natural contact between a man and a woman, the shared smiles and casual touches. After two years alone, she'd become vulnerable. Maybe even to Josh Lorenz.

She was still sorting through her feelings when Josh's daughter breezed toward the open slider. A warning from her father prompted her to step out of dusty boots, a task that she accomplished only after much hopping and tugging.

"Wow, it's Mrs. Bittner!" Carly exclaimed, once she'd gotten a clear view of her hostess. Having taken a couple of quick snapshots in the den, she barreled into the kitchen and captured Diane's image, as well. "I didn't know you lived here. You have a great vegetable garden. I can see it out my window."

"It's not in very good shape this late in the season, I'm afraid." How surprising that the girl took notice of the small patch of tomatoes, herbs and squash tucked to one side of the yard.

"I've always wanted a garden. I'd probably kill all the plants, though." The girl aimed her camera at a bowl of ripe tomatoes sitting on the counter.

Her father's forehead creased. "No, you wouldn't."

Carly adjusted her lens. "I've got a black thumb. Haven't you noticed?"

"It isn't black," he said. "It's purple."

His daughter smiled at the reference to her shade of polish. "Yeah, *this* week. Next week, who knows?"

"I'll look forward to finding out."

The pair's camaraderie touched Diane, and she appreciated that Josh had immediately countered the girl's negativity about her gardening abilities. That put a slightly more favorable light on the man.

"You're in sixth grade, right?" she asked Carly, although she already knew the answer. "My daughter's twelve, also."

"I'm still eleven. My birthday's in two weeks." Picking up a glass paperweight that had been sitting on the table, the girl studied the colored flowers inside.

"What kind of party are you planning?" Diane asked, hoping to draw her out.

"I'm too old for a party. This is beautiful. Where'd you get it?" Carly set the half globe on the counter, where it glowed in the filtered sunlight.

"My husband and I bought it in Italy on our honeymoon." Diane struggled to suppress the lump in her throat. "Venice is famous for its glassblowers."

"I'd love to go there." The girl framed the shot and clicked without using a flash. "Is your husband Italian?"

"No, he wasn't. He died," Dianne added to forestall further questions.

"Oh!" Carly lowered the camera. "I, uh…I guess I should say I'm sorry. Is that the right thing?" She glanced at her father, who nodded.

"Thank you." Diane regretted her earlier threat about revealing Josh's role on the jury. Actually, she'd prefer for everyone's sake that the fact didn't get out. "And I don't think you're ever too old for a birthday party."

Josh seized on the subject. "That's a good idea. Carly, why don't you invite some friends? We could do pizza and a movie."

"That's bo-oring."

"You've been missing your pals from La Habra. And we could invite Mrs. Bittner's daughter, Brittany."

The girl's expression clouded. "Brittany's, well…" She hesitated before concluding, "Popular."

Brittany *did* tend to be the center of a group of kids, as she'd attended Brea Academy since kindergarten. Plus she was confident and socially skilled, qualities that Carly could have used.

Despite Diane's desire to stay away from Josh, the wistfulness in his daughter's voice touched her. "Throwing a party would be a great way to expand your circle."

"I don't have a circle. Anyway, I'm not the party type." Carly didn't sound too certain about that, though.

"Parties can be tailored to the individual. For Brittany's twelfth birthday, she planned a treasure hunt at her grandmother's." Diane cherished the memory of the day. "My mom and sister helped her hide wrapped prizes all over the place. Afterward, we served homemade dessert." Noting the unguarded longing on Carly's face, she said, "I wish you'd been there. We could have used your help taking photographs."

"Yeah, maybe I should give a party where everybody else has fun and I shoot pictures." Tears glimmered in her eyes.

The last of Diane's resistance melted. "Let me think about it. Maybe I can come up with a theme for you."

"I'd appreciate that." Josh's grateful gaze warmed her. "I try to be a good dad, but this stuff's beyond me."

"You *are* a good dad." Carly hugged her father. "Don't let it go to your head."

He looped an arm around her. "I won't." To Diane, he said, "I'll remove the tree tomorrow, if that's all right."

"Fine." Impulsively, she added, "Maybe I'll have an idea for a party by then."

His daughter peered up from the shelter of his embrace. "Don't go to any trouble. Really."

"It's no trouble." This might be a way to encourage a friendship between the girls. Associating with Brittany should help to relieve Carly's outsider status at school.

Watching the father and daughter wend their way up the slope, Diane found their closeness painfully sweet. And it made her miss Will more than ever.

AT HOME, Carly disappeared into her room to upload the photos she'd just taken. After showering and changing clothes, Josh decided to check them out on her Web site. Not only was he impressed by his daughter's sense of composition, but he especially appreciated the chance to view the world through her eyes.

He slid behind the desk in his office, where the stained carpet and peeling wallpaper testified to the need for renovations. Ignoring the mess, he went online.

Carly had posted shots of the playhouse as well as the interior of Diane's home. In the den, William Bittner's framed presence confirmed the important role he still played in his family's life.

What a contrast to the way Josh felt about his ex-wife. Even though she was alive, Tiffany was virtually a stranger, her visits sporadic and her photos nonexistent except for the one that hung in Carly's room.

Josh had disposed of every other reminder of her years ago, after they'd divorced.

She'd been a personal trainer—way *too* personal when it came to a wealthy, older Newport Beach client. Perhaps she'd acted on impulse in beginning the affair, but she'd always kept her eye on the money.

When Josh and Tiffany met, he'd been too smitten to recognize just how self-involved she was. Tall and slender, with dark hair and almond-shaped eyes, Tiff had knocked Josh for a loop from the start.

A trainee with the construction company that was remodeling the house where she and her mother lived, Josh had happily performed extra chores for the stunning brunette and he'd showered her with gifts. He'd scarcely noticed that his lover always seemed preoccupied with her appearance, and when she unexpectedly became pregnant, he'd bought the most expensive engagement ring he could afford.

At first, their baby girl had delighted her. Then Carly developed into a stubborn toddler and the task of managing her fell to Josh, who took his daughter's moods in stride. Although he'd hoped for a second child, he'd accepted Tiffany's refusal to undergo another pregnancy.

Seven years into their marriage, she'd left. Seeing her with another man had been devastating, but at least she'd granted him custody of Carly.

Josh had avoided women for a while, and then he'd begun dating a blond hairdresser named Renée. Although she had a more generous personality, her refusal to discuss her past had troubled him. The more time they spent together, the more secretive she became, until they mutually decided to end the relationship.

He studied Carly's snapshot of Diane, taken in an unguarded moment. A shaft of sunlight from the window brought out the chocolate clarity of eyes touched with sadness. Although not so glamorous as Renée and Tiff, she had a narrow waist and full breasts that either of them might envy, and an inviting mouth.

Oh, for heaven's sake. Even if he *were* interested, he was the last man on earth Will Bittner's widow would look at twice.

Restlessly, Josh logged off the computer, went into the master bedroom and tied on a pair of jogging shoes. The September day had grown too warm for a run, but a power walk ought to help him burn off some nervous energy.

On the way out, he stopped by Carly's room. Set in a sunny corner, it had a great view over the Bittners' yard and beyond.

"I'm going for a walk." Out of habit, he glanced at the

computer screen in front of which his daughter sat typing. "You can reach me on my cell."

"Okay." She didn't look up.

"Who're you messaging?"

"Somebody," she muttered.

"Which somebody?"

"Somebody I know."

"From school?"

Carly's shoulders twitched. "No, Dad. Somebody I met online. He's an ax murderer who targets young girls."

He choked down a laugh. "Okay, maybe I'm overprotective, but I love you. Humor me."

Carly sighed. "I'm playing a game we have to register for and it's all supervised. I never give out personal information. All we talk about is this game. Look. You can read it, if you want." She gestured toward the screen.

He took a moment to decipher the slangy speech. The exchange *did* appear innocuous. "Thanks, honey. I'm only trying to protect you."

She chewed on a strand of purple hair and said nothing.

"Okay?" he asked.

Carly pulled the hair from her mouth. "Just spare me the lecture about all the creeps trolling the Web. I'm not an idiot."

"I know that." *But you're more naive than you think.*

Josh wondered how other single parents managed to guide their kids without smothering them. It might help if he had family members nearby for support. Josh's parents had moved to Guatemala to run an orphanage, and his former mother-in-law, a onetime Las Vegas showgirl, was a terrible influence. She'd sent his eleven-year-old daughter black lace lingerie last Christmas.

On the front porch, he inhaled the scent of freshly

mowed grass. From this high point on horseshoe-shaped Harmony Road, he could see many of the lots set around the sloping bend. The street formed the heart of Harmony Circle, a development of several hundred Mediterranean-style homes. The residents shared a clubhouse, playground and community pool and an attitude of cooperation. Most of the time, anyway.

Josh had discovered this place while overseeing a nearby remodeling job. Oliver Armstrong, a real estate agent who'd become a friend, had showed him the premises, noting the reduced price due to its run-down condition. The opportunity to fix it up and sell it at a profit in a year or so had been a strong inducement to make the move.

So here we are, Josh mused as he performed a few stretches before setting out. *Living in suburbia.* He missed his Spanish-style home in La Habra—well, a little. Although the place had had character, the single bathroom had created difficulties at morning crunch time, and he'd also been disturbed by signs of gang activity nearby.

Movement across the street at number 17 drew Josh's attention. Oliver—in his early thirties, dark-haired and quite a babe magnet—was positioning a For Sale sign on the grass under the dour supervision of the property owner, an octogenarian named Charley Lowder. With a loud *whack* from a mallet, the muscular Realtor drove the pole into the ground.

Another property on the market? Josh had only closed on this place last month. People in Southern California never seemed to stay in one place long. Of course, who was he to complain?

In a querulous tone, Charley loudly demanded, "When's the first open house?"

"Next weekend, Mr. Lowder." Oliver's tenor carried across the quiet street.

"Why not tomorrow? Like I said, I'm in a hurry. Got my first great-grandkid waiting for me."

"I've put your place on the Multiple Listing Service, so we should be getting inquiries soon," Oliver assured him.

"Well, they better be quick," the fellow said grumpily. "I want to get settled in New Mexico before Christmas."

"Let's hope it works out. There aren't any guarantees in real estate," Oliver said patiently, then gave Josh a wave.

They'd struck up a friendship after Tiffany had left Josh. Acquainted through their work, they occasionally went bowling or to a movie with Carly in tow.

Recently, the Realtor had introduced Josh and Carly to his cousin Rafe Montoya, who lived just down the street. With the twin niece and nephew that Rafe was adopting, they'd had fun attending a baseball game at Angel Stadium in Anaheim, a fifteen-minute drive away.

Oliver gave the sign a few more smacks and put away his hammer. "I'll drop off some flyers tomorrow," he told Charley.

"Fine. I ain't going nowhere except church in the morning."

The old man stumped inside. Oliver carried his tools to a sedan bearing the legend Archway Real Estate. "How's it going?" he called.

"I'm heading for a walk." Josh swung his arms to loosen his shoulders.

"Mind if I join you?"

"Not at all."

The agent's stride carried him across the street. "As long as we're out, I'd appreciate your taking a look at number 4." Oliver owned a rental property on the far side of the horseshoe, kitty-corner to Diane's place. "I'd appreciate an estimate for repairs."

"Sure thing." As owner of Lorenz Construction, Josh never

missed a chance to bring in more business. He gave Oliver a discount, since his friend steered a lot of work his way.

They set off down the street, Oliver chatting about the houses and their occupants. Cynthia Lieberman, the psychologist who lived next door to Josh, wasn't likely to move any time soon, he observed, nor was Bart Ryan, the gardening guru who lived opposite her. Roses rioting across a trellis bore testimony to his green thumb.

"Now number 13—that's been vacant for nearly a year. What a waste." The agent indicated a home whose faded stucco cried out for paint. "The owners won't even rent the place out. They're hoping their daughter will decide to live there one of these days."

"At least the yard looks good." Bart, who according to Oliver had permission to garden there, had planted a deep bed of white-on-green flowering plants.

"Yeah. Saves them paying a lawn-mowing crew," Oliver noted. "And he grows vegetables in the backyard, so it pays off for him, too."

Josh had met both Cynthia and Bart briefly in the course of his morning jogs, along with many of his other neighbors. A Chinese-American family occupied one of the houses they passed; another belonged to a fortyish African-American couple, whose small sign out front advertised a home day care center.

At the bend of the horseshoe nestled a pair of 1920s cottages that predated the rest of the development by half a century. In front of number 9, Josh spotted another For Sale sign bearing the Archway logo. "You've been busy."

"This one's a sad story," his companion confided. "It belonged to Freda Fuerte, whose sister Minnie Ortiz lives next door. They were very close. Freda passed away about six months ago, and it's taken a while to sort out the estate. As executor, Minnie hopes to sell to a nice family."

"Any prospects?"

"Yes, but the other homeowners may not be thrilled." Oliver's mouth twisted wryly. "This is actually the width of two ordinary lots, which means there's room for a mansion if someone tears down the cottage."

"Is that what your clients have in mind?"

"They're discussing the possibility."

An earsplitting roar broke the afternoon peace. From a garage down the road shot a couple of motorized scooters, whose drivers didn't look old enough to have licenses. The garage belonged to Oliver's rental house, Josh realized.

"Are those kids legal?" he asked as the duo shot past them.

"No," Oliver said with exasperation. "And as their landlord, I'm the guy who fields noise complaints. I'll have to speak to the parents."

"Problem renters, I presume."

Oliver heaved an exaggerated sigh. "The rent's usually late and I think they've sublet one of the bedrooms, in violation of their lease. On the other hand, they haven't trashed the place. You wouldn't believe the problems I had last year with my beach property down in Oceanside."

"I thought that was your private getaway."

"I rent it by the week or month. Of course, I reserve the occasional weekend for myself."

They were approaching number 4. "What kind of repairs did you have in mind?" Once Josh got a general idea, he'd return later to make a thorough evaluation and estimate.

"There's dry rot in the patio cover and cracked stucco on the side. Let's get their permission to inspect it." Oliver went to the door.

While waiting, Josh glimpsed three women next door, drinking tea at a small table in the front courtyard. Relaxing beneath the arch of a bougainvillea-draped lattice, they presented a charming picture.

He caught his breath on recognizing Diane. Angled toward him, she listened with a smile to an animated woman who bore enough resemblance to be her sister. A halo of white hair was all he could see of their mother.

In this unguarded moment, Diane seemed achingly young and fresh. He wished they'd met under less painful circumstances.

From the corner of his eye, Josh glimpsed a new figure joining the trio at number 2: Carly, with her camera in hand. And stuck in front of her face as usual. Apparently, she'd tired of surfing the Internet.

Slowly, she advanced across the sidewalk. When Diane invited her over for introductions, she hesitated and then lowered her gear.

His daughter must really like this teacher to come so far out of her shell. Although the situation between Josh and Diane might prove awkward, Carly could certainly use more adult female companionship.

One of the women gestured to a spot at the table. His daughter sat down gingerly, for all the world like a polite young miss instead of a holy terror.

Oliver finished talking to his tenant and gestured Josh into the side yard. He was turning away when he noticed Brittany stomping along the street. With a sinking sensation, Josh saw her scowl toward the interloper at her grandmother's table before struggling to hide her displeasure.

Clearly, the sweet baking maven he'd met at Diane's also had her adolescent dark side. Unhappily, Josh realized he'd been overly optimistic to hope his daughter would find new friends and a place to belong so easily.

The last thing Carly needed was more rejection. But at the moment, there wasn't a thing he could do to help her.

Chapter Three

Diane sat stunned, teacup halfway to her mouth, as her usually pleasant daughter approached Carly Lorenz. "That's *my* spot," she grumbled, as if someone had stolen her designated parking space.

"We can bring out another chair." Diane's sister, Sarah, got to her feet.

"I don't want to... Oh, suit yourself."

Even Diane's mother, Lois, whose forty-plus years of teaching had rendered her nearly shockproof, simply stared at her granddaughter's unaccustomed display of bad manners.

Carly's face grew flushed and she scooted out of the seat. "I've got homework," she mumbled, and sped off, camera swinging from her shoulder.

"See you later," Sarah called.

No response.

"Seems like a nice girl," Lois commented gently.

"I didn't mean to hurt her feelings." Brittany plopped down. "But why does she have to dress like such a dweeb?"

"Maybe she just needs a role model," Diane suggested.

"Well, I'm embarrassed to be seen with her. Don't look at me that way. It's not as if she can't help it."

Diane's spirits sank. She'd been hoping Brittany might serve as a guide for the newcomer, perhaps even take the girl under her wing. Obviously, that wasn't going to happen.

To her humiliation, she spotted Josh Lorenz watching them from the Lesters' front yard. Obviously, he'd witnessed Brittany's rude behavior and his daughter's painful retreat. Being shown in a negative light in front of him bothered her a lot.

Why? Because I've held myself up as a model of self-righteousness? For whatever reason, she hoped to change Brittany's attitude before her contempt for the hapless Carly spurred other students to imitate her. At this age, kids could be cruel.

More than once during the afternoon, Diane started to discuss the incident, but her daughter always turned pointedly away. No twelve-year-old girl appreciated having Mom critique her behavior, she reminded herself. Best to let it pass for now.

The next morning at church, she was pleased to note the sermon topic: Does the Golden Rule Still Apply in the Twenty-First Century? What an ideal opening for a conversation with her daughter about extending sympathy to an underdog.

The topic turned out to be irrelevant, however, because Brittany never heard it. Her youth group conducted a separate prayer session and then spent the rest of the morning planning a toy campaign for underprivileged kids.

How could a girl be so caring toward strangers and so unfeeling to someone who lived next door, Diane wondered later as her daughter sat on their patio cuddling Lucy. The cat flopped on its back, purring loudly enough to be heard several feet away.

Perhaps some event at school would provide a teachable moment with which to soften her daughter's heart. Now, instead, she focused on the practical. "Did you invite Suzy to dinner tonight? There's canned crab and some wonton wrappers, if you want to make crab Rangoon." The delicacy was one of Brittany's favorite things to whip up when the two friends dined together.

"What're *you* fixing?" Brittany always took an interest in the dishes Diane prepared for her monthly potluck with a group of women in the neighborhood.

They called themselves the Foxes, which stood for Females Only—Exuberantly Single. To her daughter's disappointment, youngsters weren't allowed, due to the adult content of the conversations.

"Salad with apples and walnuts." The homemade dressing included fresh lemon juice, olive oil, sugar, garlic and balsamic vinegar.

"Can you make extra for me? Suzy's tied up. I'll eat a salad and leftovers and read my new book." Sarah had given her the latest novel by Neal Shusterman, one of Brittany's favorite authors.

"Of course." Above the patio, at the top of the slope, the gate opened. A prickly sensation spread through Diane's midsection as Josh sauntered into view, one gloved hand clamped around the handle of a chain saw.

"You didn't tell me Mr. Lorenz was coming over!" The girl's voice rang with excitement.

"He called earlier and promised to chop up the tree for firewood. I wasn't sure when he'd get here." Diane preferred not to throw her daughter into the man's company. "Why don't you take Lucy to your room so the noise doesn't scare her?"

To her relief, the tactic worked. After offering a brief friendly greeting to their neighbor, Brittany scooped the cat into her arms and disappeared. Not without a couple of wistful backward glances, though.

The girl obviously hadn't considered the possibility that her hostility toward Carly might alienate Josh. How *was* Diane going to encourage the girls to become friends while keeping her distance from Carly's father?

Still, they were both mature adults. They could maintain a civil veneer. And if history was any guide, Brittany's crush would soon pass.

Her craving for a father figure previously had inspired a devotion to their church's youth pastor, but she'd recovered quickly after he departed for missionary work. More recently, she'd fixed on their neighbor, Bart Ryan, a likable gardening expert with a romantically shaggy grooming style. A couple of sessions of weeding and pruning had cured that interest, however.

Diane steeled herself as Josh approached. If she'd been thinking clearly, she'd have stayed indoors and avoided the contact. Being around him already made her intensely aware of, well, a whole lot of things she'd rather not think about.

"Apologies in advance for the noise." He set his saw on the ground. "I'll tackle the tree first, and then deal with the playhouse next weekend, if that's all right."

"Fine." Concerned that her clipped response might sound ungracious, Diane added, "I appreciate your taking care of this."

"You're welcome. If you don't mind my asking…" He cleared his throat. "I get the impression your daughter's taken a dislike to Carly."

Diane's cheeks burned at the memory of what he must have observed. "I'm sorry Carly had to deal with that. I don't know what came over Brittany."

He squared his shoulders. "I was wondering if Carly said

or did anything at school to hurt her feelings. If she needs to apologize, I'll talk to her."

The guy was willing to give Brittany that much credit rather than leaping to his own daughter's defense? Despite her profound reservations, Diane had to admire such generosity. "My kid's the one who should apologize. She isn't usually so rude."

His mouth curved sympathetically. "Seeing another girl usurp her place at the family table probably aroused some primal feelings."

"That's no excuse. She should show more self-control."

"She's just a kid. Give her a break."

Diane opened her mouth to argue, and then realized Josh was right. Perhaps she *did* expect too much of Brittany. This man had good fatherly instincts.

She wished he hadn't been involved in the trial, that she could get to know this fellow purely as a neighbor and as Carly's dad.

"It's hard for Brittany to understand how an outsider feels, I suppose," Diane admitted. "She's nearly always at the center of things."

"She seems to be a natural leader." His admiring words warmed her.

"Yes, but she takes on so much responsibility, I guess I've gotten into the habit of thinking of her as an adult," she noted. "I forget that it's normal for a sixth-grader's emotions to be in turmoil."

"I *never* forget that Carly's emotions are in turmoil," Josh commented ruefully. "They're right there on the surface."

"It must be hard for a single dad." Although a number of her students had single mothers, very few of them lived only with their fathers.

"I'd appreciate feedback about her from time to time. If

that's not asking too much." Vulnerability softened Josh's expression as he awaited her answer.

Under different circumstances, she'd have volunteered without hesitation. Torn, Diane tried to decide how to respond.

Finally, her instincts as a teacher and as a parent won out. "I'll help if I can. Your daughter's a great kid."

"Thanks."

Some instinct held Diane there for a moment, enjoying this brief peace and the gentleness of his gaze lingering on her. But she didn't dare stay. It would be inappropriate—and awkward.

Diane stood up. "I'll get out of your way and let you work."

"No hurry."

"I...have things to do. And so do you, obviously." Managing a hint of a smile, she headed indoors.

Diane felt Josh's gaze burning into her back. As she closed the sliding door, a strong physical awareness came over her, as if his arms were surrounding her from behind and his rough jaw was brushing against her neck.

Disturbed, she shook away the image. Even setting aside Josh's role on the jury, he was nothing like the man who'd been her true love since sophomore year in high school. This was no more than a temporary weakness, brought on by concern for his daughter.

In her soul, she would always be married to Will. What a kind, reliable man he'd been, handsome, in a low-key way, and so attuned to her feelings. Together, they'd created a happy world, a reality that had survived his death and eased her loneliness now.

In the den, surrounded by pictures of Will, Diane felt her tension vanish. At last she shifted her attention to a stack of fourth-grade textbooks the school was considering for use next year. She'd agreed to review them and make recommendations to the principal, Sandrine Kenton.

Analyzing the differing teaching approaches intrigued her. Yet all the while she registered the whirr of the chain saw and occasionally she found herself staring through the glass slider at the T-shirt clinging to Josh's sweaty torso. Mere curiosity, of course.

Annoyed with her inability to concentrate, she left the room. She ran a load of laundry, cleaned the bathrooms and was getting out the vacuum when she remembered that Lucy was in the house. To avoid terrorizing the cat, she mopped the front entryway instead.

At last the chain saw fell silent. Footsteps scraped and firewood clattered as a pile was made in the side yard.

Brittany sauntered down the stairs, the cat against her shoulder. "Can I put Lucy out now? She's getting restless."

Best to wait until their neighbor departed. "Hang on for another minute. There's something we should discuss."

"Okay." The girl detached a feline claw from her shoulder. "Hey! Don't cling so tightly. I won't drop you."

Gazing up lovingly, the cat meowed. Why did so many people believe cats were cold? Not in Diane's experience.

After taking a deep breath, she plunged ahead. "I know you don't care for Carly."

Brittany's face scrunched up. "She's creepy."

"She's also Mr. Lorenz's daughter. Did you realize that he saw how you treated her yesterday?" Diane warned herself to be careful about playing on Brit's desire to please the man. But for heaven's sake, an insecure girl such as Carly didn't have many defenses to pit against a class leader.

Spots of color appeared on the girl's cheeks. "He did? Was he mad?"

"No. Just concerned," Diane said. "The thing is, she's a

person, too, and she lives right behind us. Try to imagine how you'd feel if you had to start at a new school in sixth grade."

"That would be tough," came the reluctant concession. "But, Mom, why does she dress like a freak?"

"It might be a desire for attention or an attempt to show that she's her own person." Although, as a kid, Diane had usually conformed, she respected youngsters who felt a need to stand out. "Try to go easy on her, okay?"

Brit chewed her lip. "Her dad's nice, so I guess she can't be a complete loser. I'll try to be nicer."

"Thank you."

Brittany wandered toward the door with her cat. Through the window, Diane watched her daughter and Lucy emerge onto the patio.

Josh was nowhere in sight. Relieved, she washed her hands and began preparing a salad.

There was no reason they couldn't coexist as neighbors and occasionally discuss their children. Other than that, a gap would always exist between the two of them, and that was fine with Diane.

THE EIGHT WOMEN who called themselves the Foxes had begun their potlucks about a year and a half earlier. Several of them had been friends for years, but others were relatively new to the community. The group included Diane's mother and her twenty-nine-year-old sister, Sarah.

These get-togethers had begun informally when, after Will's murder, a small group of women began bringing covered dishes to Diane's house and staying for the meal. They enjoyed their shared conversations so much that Alice Watson, who'd been Diane's mentor before retiring as principal of Brea Academy, had suggested they continue meeting every month at her house next door. Although the entire community, several hundred residents strong, held its own luncheon potluck once a month at the Harmony Circle clubhouse, this was just for the one small group of friends.

Everyone had agreed. Although there'd been some discussion of rotating the event among various houses, Alice enjoyed playing hostess and everyone felt comfortable at her place.

Diane found the Foxes' companionship heartening and the harmless gossip a pleasure. Tonight, the main topic was the cottage at number 9, which eighty-eight-year-old Minnie Ortiz had put up for sale following her sister's death.

"You won't believe who looked at it on Friday," Minnie told them as she set a baking dish on Alice's granite counter. "Sherry LaSalle!"

"Seriously?" Cynthia Lieberman, a fiftyish psychologist, set out croutons alongside her lentil soup.

"That can't be good." Alice stirred the beef bourguignon in her slow cooker.

"Why not?" Minnie removed the foil from her baking dish, revealing an aromatic artichoke casserole. "She can afford it with that huge divorce settlement."

Anyone who read a newspaper in Orange County had followed the story of the stylish blonde's contentious divorce from her wealthy, older husband, who'd left her—in her late twenties, she must be over the hill by his standards—for a girl barely out of college. The fact that Elliot LaSalle had dumped his first wife for Sherry diminished sympathy for her, as did the enormous size of her lump-sum settlement. In any case, she'd wasted no time in finding a handsome new lover, a financial consultant who was in the midst of developing a Caribbean resort.

"Can you picture her living in that bungalow, cute as it is?"

Alice shook her head. "I'm betting she considers it nothing more than an investment."

"It does occupy a double lot," observed Jane McKay, an obstetrician who'd once told Diane wistfully that she doubted she'd ever have a baby of her own. "You don't suppose Sherry would tear the place down and build one of those obnoxious mansions, do you?"

To Diane, who'd grown up here, the possibility of someone removing the cottage was a personal affront. "That place is a landmark. And a mansion would be completely out of character for the neighborhood."

"Brea doesn't have a lot of buildings going back as far as the 1920s, so each one is precious," Cynthia agreed.

"I wish I could just keep the place, but I'm the executrix of my sister's estate," Minnie explained. "There are other heirs to consider, including a cousin who's having financial problems."

"Maybe she won't make an offer," Diane's mother, Lois, noted sensibly. "We're getting flustered over what-ifs and might-bes."

"Absolutely. Let's eat!" Alice urged.

The women filled their plates and settled around the dining-room table. Some time later, Alice piped up, "If you ladies don't mind, I could use your advice."

What on earth did Alice need advice about? Diane wondered. Even in her late sixties, the tall, straight-backed woman had a commanding presence that made her a dominant force on the homeowners' association board.

"Please, ask away," said Lois, who was probably the closest among them to their hostess in terms of age. Since Diane's father had died five years ago, the pair frequently attended movies and concerts together.

Alice cleared her throat. "As you know, I never married."

"You've led an amazing life, though," Diane responded loyally.

"Thanks. Well, I did nearly get married once," Alice continued. "Oh, don't look so shocked! I'm hardly a nun."

"You never told us!" Lois exclaimed.

Alice shrugged. "I'm telling you now. His name is George Tyler and we dated all through high school. He broke up with me right after graduation, a month before our wedding date."

"How cruel," Jane sympathized.

"I was terribly hurt." Alice blinked back a tear. "I used to be crazy about that boy. My goodness, I didn't realize it could still affect me."

"Did he give you a reason for breaking the engagement?" Lois asked.

Alice shrugged. "He joined the army to see the world. Later, I heard he'd married a woman he met in Germany."

"He obviously didn't deserve you. It would probably have ended badly," volunteered Tess Phipps. The divorce attorney had an aversion to marriage based on the behavior she'd seen in and out of court.

"Perhaps so." Alice took a roll from a basket and passed it along. "I'm glad I had a career. Still, it might be fun to see him again, except I'm not sure what his expectations are."

"Whoa." Lois raised her hands. "What's this about seeing him again?"

"Sounds exciting to me," observed Minnie.

"It sounds *insane*," declared Sarah. Like Tess, Diane's sister had sworn off serious relationships—in her case after a heartbreaking affair.

Alice explained that she'd run across a posting from George on a high-school reunion Web site. Now living a half dozen miles away in Whittier, he was earnestly seeking her out.

"I'll bet he has some self-serving fantasy about recapturing his lost youth." Tess sniffed.

The other women expressed varying degrees of caution and curiosity.

"If he's single now, what happened to his wife?" Cynthia inquired.

"I'm curious about that," Alice admitted. "I might e-mail him just to find out what he says."

"If you arrange a meeting, take along a few friends," Jane suggested. "They could act as buffers."

"Good idea."

The conversation moved on to other topics. Several of the women had noticed Josh working on Diane's back slope, which was visible from the street, so she explained about the fallen tree. Thank goodness she'd already told her mother and sister, who'd agreed not to mention his role in the trial to anyone. Gossip spread way too fast in Harmony Circle.

Realizing that she, too, could use some advice, Diane mentioned Carly's upcoming birthday. "I promised to try to devise a theme. Any ideas?"

"What about a scavenger hunt?" Minnie said. In this popular party game, teams canvassed the neighborhood for everyday items such as plastic spoons, rubber bands, paper clips and pencils. Whoever returned first with all the items on their list won a prize.

"Carly loves taking pictures," Sarah pointed out. "What about a *photo* scavenger hunt? They could bring back shots of the objects on their list."

"A rose bush," someone suggested.

"A dog."

"A For Sale sign."

Diane loved the notion. So did her mother, who suggested

that Brittany could bake a cake in the shape of a camera. "She loves a challenge, and it might bring the girls closer."

"That girl's the next Martha Stewart," Cynthia said, and everyone agreed.

By the time the gathering broke up, Diane felt as if she'd been inspired. She didn't even mind her mother offering to help with the party. "If it's too painful for you to be around that man."

More confusing than painful, but Diane wasn't about to share *that.* "The first shock's worn off. Now that we live back to back, I have to get used to seeing him."

"Still, he's asking a lot," Sarah insisted. "His daughter isn't your problem."

"You saw how Brittany reacted to her. I do feel responsible for smoothing that over. A little acceptance could help her a lot."

"You can help her at school. After what her father did, he has no business even talking to you," Sarah said sharply.

In some ways, Diane realized, her sister was still struggling with the loss of Will, who'd been both a mentor and a big brother to her. "I don't want Brittany to get the impression I disapprove of the Lorenzes."

"I'm proud of you for being so generous toward Carly," Lois said. "I'm sure it will work out." Before Sarah could comment, she added, "We'd better go. My favorite show's about to start."

"See you." With a smile, Diane went inside.

The house felt curiously quiet. In the kitchen, she set down the salad bowl and checked to see if Brittany had left a message. Perhaps she'd gone to Suzy's house.

There was a note, all right. *At Mr. Lorenz's. Took dessert.* She *had* promised him a slice of cake, Diane recalled.

The time on the message was forty-five minutes earlier,

longer than necessary to simply drop off the cake. Diane decided to go see what was happening. Besides, she wanted to tell Josh about the party idea.

A small shiver ran through her at the prospect of visiting his house. She shook it off. As she'd told her mother, she needed to take his presence in stride now that they were neighbors.

Carrying a flashlight, Diane slipped out the back door and headed across the grass.

Chapter Four

"You don't *always* use paper, do you?" Brittany Bittner asked Josh as she tucked crumb-strewn disposable plates into a trash bag.

Sitting in his curtainless kitchen, Josh, Carly and their guest had each enjoyed a slice of rich chocolate cake, topped with vanilla ice cream from the freezer. Ice cream was one of the few culinary staples he kept in good supply, along with canned soup and frozen dinners. On a good week, he might also remember to pick up a bag of prepared salad, but often it withered in the refrigerator before he or Carly thought to eat it.

His daughter hadn't said much since Brittany had arrived. Mostly she'd watched with a wary expression as the other girl chattered up a storm.

"Well, we do have those plastic dishes." He indicated one of the open cabinets.

"They're *stained*." Brittany's nose wrinkled. "Not that I'm criticizing."

"Yes, you are," Carly said.

Josh cringed. "If she is, I deserve it. We live sort of a gypsy existence around here."

"I figured gypsies would have exotic china. I mean, stuff they collect on their travels." Brittany sighed. "I'm not being very practical, am I? I suppose rattling around in their painted wagons would break everything." She rushed on. "Do you like goulash? I think that's what gypsies eat. I have a great recipe for it."

Was this kid really only twelve? She'd already offered them detailed advice on saving money with coupons, rotating canned goods and checking the expiration dates, and on... Well, Josh couldn't remember all of it.

Uh-oh. She'd stopped speaking, and now the three of them were sitting there blankly. The subject, he recalled, was goulash. "I think I ate some once," he ventured. "I'm sure it wasn't as good as yours."

"I'll fix it for you sometime."

"Great."

They'd exhausted *that* subject. Flashing him a quick smile, Brittany moved on. "Why is there a hole in the wall to the dining room?"

"He told you already," Carly grumbled.

"I know... Something about a serving window. But why go to all that trouble?" she persisted, her attention fixed on Josh. As her mom had said, the girl clearly craved a father figure.

Josh was touched but a little intimidated, too. He could barely parent his own daughter, let alone deal with this miniature Betty Crocker.

However, while he might not find much to say on most other subjects, renovation was his specialty. "It'll be great for casual entertaining. The host and hostess can talk to their guests while they're working in the kitchen."

"What about the noise? I mean, from the dishwasher, while they're eating?"

Sharp kid, he thought. "I'll install a clear sliding panel."

She absorbed that information with a flick of the eyelashes. "So once you've renovated, you're going to throw a lot of parties?"

Carly shuddered. "Ugh. Parties!"

Their guest paid no heed. "I want to be a caterer. Maybe you could hire me."

"I'd love to hire a caterer," Josh agreed. "But as for our future plans…"

Outside, the automatic sensor lights activated. A moment later, Diane crested the slope and opened the gate between their properties.

"Your mom's here to fetch you." He stood up, hoping his neighbor wasn't in too big a hurry to collect her daughter.

Despite their obvious differences, he found Diane a pleasure to be around. And not necessarily because of the tantalizing picture she made with that sweater clinging to her figure, either, or the way her full lips parted from the exertion of her trek across the backyard. He'd never met a beautiful woman with more inner strength or more kindness, he thought.

Better keep a lock on your thoughts, mate. That's forbidden territory.

She spotted the three of them. When Brittany went to the sliding door, he feared the Bittners might simply leave.

To his relief, Diane stepped inside. "Am I intruding?"

"Not at all."

Visualizing the place through her eyes, Josh felt a bit embarrassed. In the den, he'd ripped decrepit fixtures out of the wall and ceiling and had left unpainted splotches of plaster in their place. He'd also stripped off the carpet and pad, exposing a cement floor that was now strewn with a couple of scatter rugs.

"Welcome to the land of Before," he said.

Diane peered around the den. "The renters who used to live here seemed nice. I didn't realize they'd trashed the place."

"They didn't. But the house is thirty years old, and apparently nobody ever bothered to replace anything. I'm in the middle of it." He shot a warning glance at Carly, who was reaching for her camera, as usual. For heaven's sake, Diane ought to be able to drop by without having her picture show up on the Internet thirty minutes later.

His daughter subsided, fingers twitching.

"My best friend lived here when I was growing up. Nancy Yoshida." Wistfully, Diane surveyed the partly dismantled kitchen. "Of course, we didn't own the house I'm in now. I lived at my mom's place. The Yoshidas moved away after Nancy and her brother grew up."

"I can tell you miss them." He hadn't realized Diane had spent her formative years in this neighborhood.

"We keep in touch."

Josh hadn't stayed in contact with anyone from high school, but then his family had moved from one apartment to another in the central part of Orange County, so he'd changed schools often. Like his parents, he'd been preoccupied with his brother's long illness, but now he wished he'd been able to put down roots as a kid.

That was his goal for Carly. He regretted being unable to accomplish it sooner, and felt in a hurry to renovate and sell this place so they could move on to what he thought of as Step Three. That was his dream of a place that met all their needs, with enough land to stretch out and feel like rulers of their own castle.

"How were the Foxes?" Brittany asked her mother.

"Oh, the usual." Diane didn't seem eager to discuss the matter.

"Who're the Foxes?" Josh ventured. "Was this an animal rescue mission?"

Diane laughed. "It's a group of ladies. Just a silly title we gave ourselves." She turned to Carly. "They helped me come up with a theme for your birthday party. I hope you don't mind."

Carly gave a shrug, her usual response to unpleasant or embarrassing topics.

"What are you talking about?" Brittany demanded. "What birthday party?"

His daughter seemed to shrink into her oversized black sweatshirt. "Nothing. Don't worry about it."

Diane glanced from one girl to the other. Josh half expected her to drop the subject, but she persevered. "Carly's birthday is coming up. I thought she might like the idea of a party with a photography theme. We could rustle up digital cameras for the guests to use and stage a photo scavenger contest."

Josh liked the sound of this. It would allow Carly to hide behind a lens and be part of a group at the same time. "What do you think?" he asked her.

"I don't know." If she retreated any further, she'd disappear completely inside her sweatshirt like a turtle in its shell.

Brittany's forehead furrowed. "You're throwing her a birthday party?" she asked her mother dubiously.

One look at Carly's trembling lower lip told Josh how badly the implied objection stung. Much as he respected Diane's good intentions, this had gone far enough. Perhaps too far. For whatever reason, Brittany disliked his daughter, and Carly had already suffered more than enough rejection in her life. "It was kind of you to take an interest, but I think we'll pass. Brittany, thanks for the cake."

"You're welcome. Oh, I forgot my plate." She went to the counter to collect her cut-glass serving dish.

To Josh, Diane mouthed the words, "I'm sorry."

"It was worth a try."

In a louder voice, she said, "You can still use the theme.

I'm sure one of the bakeries in town could create a cake in the shape of a camera. Also, you could try doing something clever with your snacks, like making frames of carrot sticks."

"Mom!" Brittany finished rinsing the plate. "Nobody eats carrot sticks at a birthday party. I could come up with much better snack ideas, and no bakery is going to go to all the trouble of shaping a cake like a camera unless they already have a mold. Which they probably don't."

"I'm sure the Lorenzes can handle this without our help," Diane said earnestly.

"Don't be silly," Brittany persisted. "This calls for an expert."

Carly stared in confusion from mother to daughter. Then Josh caught the hint of a smile as she worked out Diane's psychology.

Brittany obviously recognized it as well. "Yeah, I get it. You're maneuvering me. But if they're going to do this, they ought to do it right."

"The way you bake is amazing," Carly volunteered.

Josh wanted to hug her. What a brave thing to say. It put her in a risky position, practically asking for a sharp retort.

Diane, who must have shared the same thought, appeared to be holding her breath.

"Okay, I'll pitch in," Brittany said. "If you'll invite Suzy, too."

"Sure." Carly went further. "If you're looking for ideas, why don't you come upstairs and check out my equipment? I've got filters and a tripod, and interchangeable lenses to shoot super closeups. Maybe you could duplicate some of them in food."

Brittany tapped one foot, like a teacher lost in thought. "I didn't realize you had that much gear. Do you think you could photograph my cakes for an ad?"

"Sure."

"What kind of ad?" Diane asked.

"Just something I've been thinking about." To Carly, she said, "Let's go!"

Josh's daughter galloped out of the room with Brittany on her tail. Was it possible the pair had found something in common? His spirits rose.

"Thank you," he said.

"You're welcome."

He felt a surge of warmth for both their daughters. And gratitude for Diane's assistance, of which he could have used a whole lot more. "As long as you're here, would you mind consulting with me about the party? I'm a rank amateur at these things."

"What can I do?" She clasped her hands.

"For one thing, this den's a mess. Do you think we can keep Carly's guests corralled in the living room? I haven't torn that up too badly yet."

"How many girls do you think she'll invite?"

"Half a dozen at most."

"No problem." She considered for a moment. "Or you could reserve the neighborhood clubhouse." The community facility overlooked a large pool. "I haven't heard of any events scheduled a week from Saturday, so it might be available. The following weekend is the homeowners' picnic and pool party. You did hear about that, didn't you?"

"Oliver mentioned it." Josh hadn't paid much attention, since he didn't plan to get any more involved in Harmony Circle than necessary.

He was only staying for a year or so, not long enough to merit putting down roots. Once he'd fixed up the present house and sold it for a profit, he could finally construct the place he'd been longing for since childhood. A place where

Carly would never have to feel like an outsider, where she could have the horse she'd always dreamed of, and which would have space on the grounds for a retirement cottage for his parents.

On the other hand, a picnic sounded like fun—especially if Diane was there. "Maybe we'll go for the picnic part. Carly refuses to swim, though. She won't even let me buy her a swimsuit."

Diane smiled sympathetically. "At her age, she's probably self-conscious about her body. Maybe her mom could take her shopping."

It must be hard for a woman who exuded caring to understand a mother such as Tiffany. "My ex-wife's interest in our daughter tends to be erratic." That was the most diplomatic phrasing Josh could manage.

"I'll talk to her at the party. Surely she wants her daughter to have a swimsuit. This is southern California, where girls practically live at the pool and the beach in the summer."

"I'll make sure we invite her." He rather hoped Tiff wouldn't show up, though, not so much because of her own self-absorbed personality but because she might bring along her mother. Flora could singlehandedly disrupt any event short of a Las Vegas showgirl convention.

Diane began to pace. "I hope I don't seem too interfering. Honestly, Josh, I'm not trying to take over your life. It's just that Carly brings out the mother hen in me."

"It's great. She needs that." Remembering her comment about Brittany seeking a father figure, he considered offering his help in return, but decided that might spoil the delicate peace between them. Instead, he pointed to the rug Diane was approaching. "Watch for the loose edge."

"What?"

"The edge sticks up. I'd hate for you to trip."

"Oh." She stared down. "Doesn't living like this get uncomfortable for you? With everything torn up, I mean."

"No. I don't see what's here, I see what's *going* to be here," Josh explained. "Hardwood floors. Oak cabinets with revolving shelves. A walk-in pantry."

"That sounds beautiful."

"It will be."

They'd entered his comfort zone—remodeling. "Would you like to see more of what I'm doing?"

For an anxious moment, he feared she might decide to leave instead. Then the girls' voices drifted downstairs, eager and absorbed, reminding them both that they weren't alone. "Sure, just a quick tour before I collect Brittany. There's school tomorrow."

"Suits me. Let's start with the living and dining rooms." He led her through the front, outlining future improvements. From there, they mounted the staircase, for an overview of the cathedral-ceilinged space.

As Josh detailed his plans, he heard Brittany comment, "That rose looks larger than life, and your focus is amazing. Each dewdrop stands out. I can practically count them."

Prickliness had given way to admiration, at least temporarily. Josh and Diane exchanged pleased glances.

"It's a little sentimental," Carly countered. "Now, here's an interesting shot. What do you think?"

"Wow! I can't believe you shot a zit on somebody's nose."

Josh chuckled and Diane shook with laughter. Only a sixth-grader would pick a subject like that, he reflected.

"At least you can't tell whose nose it is," Carly noted.

"Sure you can," Brittany said. "It's Nick Salonica's. He's in Mom's class. I'd recognize his nose anywhere!"

"Oops. I'll take it off the Web site before anyone else sees it," came the abashed response.

Diane's eyes widened. "That's on a Web site?"

"I'll make sure she deletes it," Josh promised.

"Who's out there?" Carly called, as if there could be any doubt. "Are you guys snooping?"

Diane stepped into the open doorway. "Sorry to interrupt, girls, but it's getting late."

From behind her, Josh surveyed the cheerful hodgepodge of his daughter's room. Photos were tacked onto almost every available surface, a tripod occupied one corner and clothes lay scattered on the chair and floor. The bed sported a lacy pink-and-white spread with matching pillows, a gift from Carly's mother, while across the window stretched midnight-blue curtains festooned with stars and moons. Those had been Carly's choice.

"Sorry for the mess," his daughter told Diane.

"That's what we get for dropping by uninvited," she replied cheerfully.

"Oh, it always looks like this."

Diane laughed. "I appreciate your honesty."

"Things get torn and stained if they're not cared for," Brittany advised. "You wouldn't treat your camera equipment that way, would you?"

"Good point." Carly clicked off the Web site. "Better be careful. You don't want to become a good influence, do you?"

Brittany grinned. "See you at school."

"You bet."

With a farewell to Josh, the Bittners whisked down the stairs and out the sliding door.

Josh lingered in his daughter's doorway. "I'm glad you guys had a good time."

"She's nice. Like her mom," Carly said wistfully. "I'll probably manage to tick her off in a day or so. I have a gift for that."

"Don't run yourself down." Crossing to the desk, Josh gave his daughter a hug. "You're a sweetheart."

"I'm glad my father thinks so, anyway," she replied.

"Indeed, I do. We're just independent types, you and me."

"That's for sure!"

When Carly returned to her Web site, deleting the offending photo, Josh took his cue and wandered out. On the landing, he caught a lingering whiff of Diane's scent.

He had liked having her beside him. To joke with, to consult, to share observations.

Still, as he'd told Carly, they were both essentially loners. The cozy, old-fashioned, deep-rooted Bittner family was about as different from the Lorenzes as any family could be.

All the same, he intended to enjoy this peace with his neighbors while it lasted. For Carly's sake, and maybe his own as well.

BRITTANY EYED Diane while flipping through favorite recipes on the counter. "No gloating."

"Wouldn't dream of it." Diane tucked some lesson plans into her briefcase, organizing her papers for the week ahead.

"You brought up that business about the cake because you figured I couldn't resist." The girl shoved a strand of hair off her face. "Well, there's a method to my madness. Next weekend I'm going to bake my first wedding cake.

"I'm not saying I can do as well as the chefs on the Food Channel, but I'm pretty good. After Carly photographs it, I'll take out an ad in the PTA newsletter."

"Wedding cake?" Diane looked at her daughter with mingled pride and alarm. Despite the endless references to a catering career, Diane hadn't expected Brittany to try to become an entrepreneur quite this young. "Honey, a wedding is the most special day of people's lives. If anything went wrong with the cake, it would be awful. Why don't you start with some holiday baking? You fixed fabulous pumpkin cupcakes last year, and your carrot-cake bars are superb."

"I suppose that would be all right. I could bake an assortment that shows my range." Wistfully, Brittany regarded the cookbook she was holding in her hands. "Wedding cakes are top of the heap, though. If you can master them, you can do anything."

"So Carly's going to help you out?" Diane prodded.

"We're helping each other. I mean, with her party."

"I'm glad you've found some common ground," Diane ventured.

If she thought she'd won the battle, however, she quickly learned otherwise.

"Couldn't she do something about her hair? I heard one boy at school say she won't need a costume for Halloween."

"That's cruel. Also, he could get into trouble for mocking another student." Brea Academy had a strict policy against that.

"Mom, I kind of like her, but you can't expect me to defend her all the time. She has to meet the other kids halfway."

Diane supposed that was true. "She'll find her own balance eventually. Please encourage the other kids to give her a break."

"I'll try." Her daughter eyed the discarded Sunday paper, which Diane had set aside to recycle, and plucked out a booklet of coupons. "Mom, you were supposed to save these."

"I thought that was an ad." Guiltily, Diane reflected that she ought to pay more attention to such things. Much as she appreciated the need to scrimp, she couldn't muster the same enthusiasm for the habit as her daughter.

The twelve-year-old spread the booklet on the table.

"Here's a whole dollar off my favorite salsa. Fifty-five cents on toilet paper. We're running low, by the way."

"I'm glad you keep track of these things."

"Somebody has to."

"When did we ever run out?" Diane teased.

"I recall a couple of last-minute runs to the store," Brittany joked.

"That's mostly for your baking."

"I can't always be sure which recipe I'm going to use. Hey, look. Buy one get one free on apple juice." Happily distracted, the girl snipped away with a pair of scissors.

How many children in wealthy Orange County grew up appreciating the value of a dollar? Still, Diane wished she earned enough so that neither of them had to do this. If Will were alive…

Suddenly, she missed him almost beyond bearing. Missed his protection, his optimism, his steadying presence. The playful twists of his grin. Being pulled onto his lap to snuggle. She lowered her face to hide her emotions and control a threatened flow of tears.

During the first year after his death, she'd wept on a daily basis. Since then, the intensity had lessened, but occasional bouts of grief still struck without warning.

Guiltily, Diane recalled standing near Josh tonight atop the stairs, listening to the girls. How tempting it was to let down her guard and get close to a man simply because he lived nearby and seemed to be a good father. But that wasn't fair to Will's memory, and it wasn't fair to her, either.

Silently, she conceded a point she'd been trying to deny until now—that she felt drawn to Josh. How had this happened? How could she have feelings for the man who'd deprived Will of justice?

Surely the temptation stemmed from proximity and lone-liness, nothing more. Her grief counselor had warned her that she'd go through transitional stages. This susceptibility must be one of them.

With luck, it would soon pass.

Chapter Five

The subcontractor had done an excellent job of installing the Spanish-influenced tile, Josh observed on Tuesday as he walked through a newly remodeled patio with his client. The house, in the town of Yorba Linda, offered a splendid canyon view, which the homeowners could enjoy even more fully now that their place included a heated spa and an outdoor kitchen facility.

"We love it," the woman enthused. "We'll certainly be recommending Lorenz Construction to our friends."

"Thank you." Josh crossed off several more items on his checklist, then stooped to grab a stray bit of paper. "Can't be leaving trash behind." He insisted that his crews clean up after themselves. "Everything seems to be in order, but please call me if there are any problems."

"We will. And thanks."

"Mind if I take some photos for our records?"

"Not at all."

With a small camera he retrieved from his truck, Josh shot the completed work, using the same angles he'd used for his "before" shots. These would join others posted at his office and on his Web site. He might not have his daughter's photographic talent, but he knew well enough how to frame a shot for good effect.

On the point of leaving, Josh paused to savor the overall effect of the patio. It deserved inclusion in a magazine, he reflected with pride.

He made mental notes of the features that particularly appealed to him: the archway separating the pool area from the dining room and the artist-designed railing atop a low stone wall bordering the property. He would try similar elements on his 3-D computer model of the home he was designing for him and Carly.

Josh, his parents and Carly would form their own community, a place where his daughter could feel secure. There'd be no homeowners' association to lay down rules, and no pressure, internal or financial, to move again.

His cell phone rang just as he was getting into the truck. "Lorenz Construction. Josh speaking," he answered.

"Mr. Lorenz?" asked an authoritative woman's voice. "This is Sandrine Kenton at Brea Academy."

The principal. "Is my daughter all right?"

"Carly's fine," Dr. Kenton said. "There's been a bit of a misunderstanding, that's all. Can you join us?"

"Right now?" He'd intended to swing by another job site before grabbing lunch.

"I'd appreciate it."

"I'll be there." Thinking quickly, Josh rearranged the rest of his schedule. He wondered what was wrong. Had Carly gotten into an argument with another girl or offended a teacher with her bluntness?

Fifteen minutes later, he pulled into the school parking lot. Situated between a residential neighborhood and a shopping center, the tree-shaded campus included a groomed playing field and a series of one-story stucco buildings.

Josh had believed Carly would blossom in smaller classes here, where students received personal attention, and he'd been impressed by the school's reputation for academic excellence. And the cost hadn't been too bad once Tiffany had persuaded her husband to pay half. Al Finley wasn't stingy— Josh had to give him that.

All the same, perhaps his confidence in the school was misplaced. Although Carly liked her teachers, she described her fellow students as cliquish. Still, classes hadn't been in session long. Already, she and Brittany seemed to be reaching an accord.

He felt a spurt of anticipation at the possibility of running into Diane while he was here. Then, recalling the reason he'd come, Josh quickened his pace as he approached the administration building.

In the principal's outer office, Josh found Carly slumped in a chair, arms crossed, her expression sullen. At the counter, an older boy and girl, whose badges indicated they were eighth-grade student helpers, sat collating papers. Their cleancut demeanor made a marked contrast to his daughter's messiness. Was there even a slight chance she might achieve that level of maturity by their age?

"Hey," Josh said. Carly shifted position to acknowledge him. "What's going on?"

"Everybody's paranoid," she muttered.

"About what?"

Before she could answer, the secretary signaled them. "Mr. Lorenz? Dr. Kenton's expecting you. Carly, you may go in also."

"Thanks." He held the door for his daughter, who trudged inside and plopped into a corner chair.

Dr. Kenton, a stocky woman with upswept gray hair, circled around from behind her desk to shake hands. "I appreciate
your dropping by."

Josh replied with appropriate civility. As soon as they were
seated, the principal came to the point. "Another student complained that Carly brought her camera into the girls' locker
room. For obvious reasons, we have strict policies against
taking photographs there."

"I didn't shoot anybody in their underwear," Carly flared.
"It's safer to store my camera in my gym locker than my regular
locker. Those are outdoors, where anybody could break in."

Josh glanced inquiringly at the principal. "Did you check
the camera?"

"Yes, with her permission. There weren't any objection-
able photos," Dr. Kenton confirmed. "However, the other girl
claimed she deleted them."

"I didn't," Carly grumbled. Then she added, "Lots of girls
have cameras in their cell phones. They put *them* in their gym
lockers all the time. The tattletale just *assumed* I used it."

"Sounds as if it's one person's word against the other's.
Were there any witnesses?" Josh braced himself for the most
probable reply, that no one chose to speak on behalf of an
outsider.

"Actually, yes," the principal replied, to his surprise. "A
third girl took me aside to say your daughter had stored the
camera directly in the locker without taking any pictures.
That's resolved the matter for now."

"Just like I said," Carly groused. "I did nothing wrong."

"While that appears to be true, girls at this age tend to be
hypersensitive about their bodies," Dr. Kenton said. "We share
their concern, especially these days, when pictures can turn
up on the Internet."

"I'd never upload anything like that," Carly objected.

Not intentionally. Josh recalled his daughter's posting of the pimply nose in the belief its owner couldn't be identified. "Thank goodness for the witness."

"It was Brittany," Carly said.

"That was kind of her. More than kind. Brave." Young girls could be vicious, and Diane's daughter had nothing to gain by speaking up for an unpopular newcomer.

"Brittany's an outstanding young lady. So is Carly. However, that still leaves us with an issue," the principal said. "Brea Academy doesn't bar girls from carrying cameras on campus, but this almost constant photographing of others has become an issue. Therefore, I suggest a moratorium."

"What's that?" Carly asked suspiciously.

"A break," the principal clarified. "I'd like you to leave your camera at home for a week. After that, we'll discuss ground rules for bringing it again."

Carly leaped to her feet. "That's just mean. Dad, get me out of here. I want to go to a *real* school!"

He couldn't allow her to insult the principal for trying to sort out a difficult situation. "Dr. Kenton is not being mean." Furthermore, the camera might be interfering with Carly's ability to make friends.

"I'm sorry," his daughter muttered. "But I want to transfer."

None of the parenting books Josh had read had prepared him for this situation. Still, a man who could face down laggard suppliers, slow-moving subcontractors and an otherwise united jury ought to be able to handle a moody sixth-grade girl. Even if her eyes *were* demanding that he prove his loyalty by taking her side.

"Public schools might be even less flexible about your camera," he cautioned. "And how do you suppose Brittany's going to feel if you leave after she stood up for you?"

Carly opened her mouth to argue, and then stopped. "I didn't think of that," she admitted meekly.

Dr. Kenton stepped into the breach. "How about if Carly continues to bring the camera, but checks it with me each morning? When we have an assembly or special event, she can serve as my official photographer. I'd love to have more pictures for our Web site and yearbook."

In this way, Carly could maintain her identity as a photographer, yet fulfill a socially acceptable role. "That's a great idea. Right?"

She stared at the floor. "Okay." The response wasn't exactly gracious, but at least she was going along with the plan.

Josh and the principal shook hands, and a shared look of understanding passed between them. Josh was relieved to sense that he had an ally in helping his daughter weather this difficult period.

For that day, they agreed that he should take the camera home, and Carly didn't object. So he slung the strap over his shoulder, waited while the secretary wrote a pass allowing his daughter to return to class, and accompanied her into the hall. "Are you okay?"

"I'm fine." Normal reticence had replaced her earlier anger.

"Is there something else I should have done?" Josh pressed.

"You were okay," she conceded.

"Not brilliant?"

A tiny smile emerged. "Dad, you didn't mess up. Don't fish for compliments."

When he reached for a hug, she dodged and took off. Too grown up for public displays of affection, Josh supposed. With a heart full of love, he watched his daughter speed toward an exit.

All that defiant multicolored hair. The too-large gloomy clothing. Was this the child who only yesterday had flung herself into his arms at every opportunity? Yet she could still be delightful, too. Much as he wished that Tiffany cared more, he was glad he was entrusted with raising their child.

Just as he was about to leave, Josh overheard a loud male voice through the open office door. A man was addressing the secretary in an irritated tone. "I'm on my lunch break and I need to speak to Mrs. Bittner now."

"I believe she's with students."

"Nonsense. My son's in her class, and they go to the music room at eleven on Tuesdays and Thursdays. She's probably sitting there with her feet up, buffing her nails."

Josh felt his temper rising. The man had no business making ridiculous accusations about Diane.

"Is this something Dr. Kenton can handle?" the secretary asked with strained patience.

"It's about the grade she gave my son. If I ask the principal, she'll just tell me to speak to the teacher," he snapped.

If this man's son resembled him at all, the kid probably deserved a low grade, Josh thought. But of course children weren't to blame for their parents' behavior.

Finally, the woman yielded. "Very well, Dr. Salonica. Here's a pass. I'll phone to let Mrs. Bittner know you're coming."

Salonica. The name rang a bell. Oh, yes, the orthodontist who ran Smile Central, where Carly got her braces. For which Josh paid the enormous bills.

Sure enough, he recognized the balding man who barreled out of the office and down the hall. Dr. Salonica didn't seem to notice Josh following quietly in his wake.

It might be bending the school rules to wander around without a pass, Josh supposed, but he *had* checked in at the office. Besides, he meant to stand by, in case Diane needed help with this overbearing father.

Childish laughter and a teacher's voice drifted through open windows. The primary classrooms were located at the center of the campus, with upper grades toward the rear of the grounds and the cafeteria and gymnasium along either side.

Josh surveyed the fresh paint and neat landscaping. The roofs appeared in good condition, too. While the grounds mattered less than the quality of instruction, they confirmed an efficiently run organization.

A short distance ahead, Dr. Salonica yanked open a door and marched into a classroom. As Josh approached, he could hear the man fuming.

"Nick deserved better than a B on his water-preservation poster," the orthodontist claimed. "He does beautiful work. That poster's practically a professional job."

In a measured tone that gave Josh a tingle of pleasure, Diane responded, "That poster *is* outstanding, Dr. Salonica. With, I presume, a lot of help from you or your wife."

"Yes, we assisted him. That's a parent's job. You're punishing our son for that?" he demanded.

"A B isn't a punishment." Her patient voice was firm. "I approve of parents working with their children, and I certainly don't grade down for it. But despite the beautiful rendering, your son illustrated the water cycle without showing how it affects animals and people—which was the assignment. That's why his poster doesn't merit an A."

Drawing closer, Josh could see the orthodontist scrutinizing other posters arrayed on the wall. From this angle, he could make out only Diane's shoulder and the back of her head.

"You gave *that* childish thing an A?" Dr. Salonica pointed at something Josh couldn't see.

"The student who produced that followed directions and

showed a lot of creativity," she shot back. "Do you want me to punish him for *not* having his parents do part of his work?"

"My son is Ivy League material. I expect his grades to reflect that."

As the man continued to protest, Josh sauntered into the room. A whiff of chalk and the smell of gym shoes carried him back to his own school days in a small desert town. He'd enjoyed that place until his brother's illness had forced the family to move closer to major medical facilities.

Diane's startled expression brought him back to the present. Seated on the edge of her desk in the middle of her domain, she seemed larger than life. Vaguely, he noted the books crowded on shelves, the desktop computers and the maps festooning one wall. Mostly, he felt energy flowing from Diane.

She held her head high, unfazed by her visitor. Really, she didn't require rescuing, Josh realized. All the same, he appreciated the chance he had to give her a little boost.

"Hi." Extending his hand, he introduced himself to the orthodontist, who regarded him dourly. "My daughter's one of your patients."

With a visible effort, the man shifted to a friendlier tone. "Oh, yes. Good to see you."

Josh deliberately let the man assume both their children were in Diane's class. "So your son has Mrs. Bittner. What a stroke of luck!"

"Yes. Of course, the semester's just started, so I can hardly say whether…"

"Everyone says she's strict, but that's what it takes to prepare these kids for what lies ahead. SATs and AP tests and all that. It's never too early to establish high standards, don't you think?" Josh continued.

The arrow hit its mark. "Certainly. My daughter's a freshman in high school and thanks to Brea Academy she's at the top of her class."

"Exactly!" Josh assumed a waiting stance as if he, too, wanted to discuss his child's progress with the teacher.

"Well." The orthodontist cleared his throat. "Yes, I'll definitely talk to Nick Jr. about listening to his assignments more carefully."

"He's a bright young man," Diane assured the father. "I'm sure we'll have a great year."

Mollified, Dr. Salonica took his leave. Josh stuck his head out the door and watched the fellow vanish from sight. "Whew. He's gone."

"He's not lurking around listening to other people's conversations, like someone I could mention?" Diane teased.

"Did I do that?"

"Yes, and thank heaven." She burst out laughing. "That was priceless."

"I never realized how much teachers have to put up with."

"It's too bad our educational system places more emphasis on grades than on whether the child's learned anything, although marks can be great motivators." She dusted chalk off her hands. "What brings you here?"

Josh explained about the locker incident. "Please thank Brittany for both of us."

"I'm glad she spoke up." Through the windows, the midday light brought out green flecks in Diane's brown eyes. Here on home turf, she seemed relaxed and glowing with confidence.

Another thought occurred to Josh. "By the way, please ask her to keep track of everything she spends baking for the party. I insist on reimbursing her. In fact, I'd like to pay for her time."

Diane shook her head. "She won't charge for doing a friend

a favor. Besides, Carly's photographs of her baking will be ample repayment. She's quite talented."

"Talented, but not always discreet," he commented wryly. "By the way, she's very excited about the party. Three of her friends from La Habra are coming and bringing their cameras."

"I'm glad to hear that. What about food—any ideas?"

"Well, you can't go wrong with pizza." He hadn't actually given the matter much consideration. "I must be overlooking some details. What else do we need?"

"Themed plates and decorations are always nice."

"Oh, right." When Carly was younger, he'd simply booked a child-oriented fun center and let the staff handle everything. This was *way* more complicated. "I'll see if I can find some."

"And don't forget the goody bags," Diane prompted.

Did some cosmic party planner concoct these ideas just to befuddle single fathers? "You stuff them full of toys, right? Wait—the girls are too old for toys."

Amusement played across her face. "You need a personal shopper."

"I'd kill for a personal shopper."

"We should take the girls to the party store," she announced. "They'll have a ball, and we can do some shopping."

"There's such a thing as a party store?" That was news to him.

"Right here in Brea. How about Saturday afternoon?" she asked. "Brittany's church group has a meeting earlier, but she should be free by three."

If they hadn't been standing in full view of anyone passing by, Josh would have kissed her. The woman had just saved his life.

"That would be awesome," he said, not quite certain whether he was referring to her invitation or to the prospect of kissing her.

"You did remember to buy your daughter a present, didn't you?" Diane's question brought him down to earth with a jolt.

Fortunately, he *had* thought of that. "I ordered some photographic editing software she's been lusting after," Josh said. "It should arrive in plenty of time."

"Then we're set."

"A thousand thanks. Possibly a million."

"My pleasure."

That was his cue to depart. To march out of the classroom and leave her in peace.

"Is there something else?" She watched him curiously.

"I just…" Josh caught the babble of childish voices, heading this way. The kids must have finished their music lesson. He'd better hurry. "I just want to say that you are the ultimate wise woman, steeped in the mysteries of parenthood and astoundingly generous with a lunk like me. And if Dr. Salonica gives you any more grief, I'll personally pop him one."

"Oh, I can handle him." Sliding off the edge of the desk, she brushed her skirt as she prepared to face the students. "See you Saturday."

"Wouldn't miss it." He skimmed down the steps and took an alternate route toward the parking lot to avoid swimming upstream through a sea of students.

An unaccustomed sense of well-being buoyed Josh all the way to his car.

Chapter Six

Purple, lavender and rose. A gorgeous blend of colors swirled through the crocheted squares that were loosely assembled on the table in Diane's mother's dining room. Her sister, Sarah, tucked her chestnut hair behind one ear as she tried one arrangement of finished squares, then another.

Diane flexed her fingers, which were stiff after a half hour crocheting alongside Lois and Sarah, working on an afghan to raise funds for a women's shelter. It would be sold alongside a variety of other handmade craft items at their church's pre-Christmas fair.

Diane's motivation in suggesting this project during the summer had been as much to spend time with her mother and sister as to support a worthy cause. Although living across the street from her family allowed frequent contact, their casual conversations too often remained at a superficial level.

She'd cleared this Thursday evening, knowing Brittany would be doing homework at Suzy's. Nearing their goal, the three women had each crocheted a square already and were taking a break before completing another set. Then Sarah would finish tinkering with the design, and next week they'd connect the whole thing together.

More importantly, Diane was catching up on the latest developments in her sister's job search. A public relations executive at a small firm, Sarah had been trying to leave her present job since the breakup of an affair with her boss the previous year. Hundreds of résumés had gone out, but the only job offers she'd received so far were either too far away or they didn't pay enough.

"What happens if you don't find something soon?" Diane asked as she broke into a chocolate-chip muffin.

"I've been thinking about starting my own business, but my stomach gets tied in knots at the prospect. I guess I'm just not a risk-taker," Sarah admitted. "Maybe I'll stay put. At least then I can keep the clients I've brought in."

"What about Rick?" That was Sarah's boss. A divorced man in his late thirties, he'd gone after Sarah with gifts and expensive outings, hinted at marriage and then dumped her without an explanation. Eventually, she'd discovered he had a pattern of serial dating, leading women along and then dropping them for a new challenge.

Lois brought mugs of hot apple juice from the kitchen. "You'll find the right solution. All this waiting and struggling has to be for a reason."

Sarah took one of the mugs. "You're a hopeless optimist, Mom."

"Isn't that a contradiction in terms?" Diane teased.

"Precisely," their mother said. "I've never met a hopeless optimist."

"Oh, please." Sarah took a sip and then said, "Mom, tell her about Alice."

"Changing the subject, are we?" Lois raised an eyebrow.

"What about Alice?" Diane demanded. "Does this concern that fellow, George?"

Lois nodded. "She e-mailed him, and they talked on the phone. Turns out he's a retired civil engineer and widowed. He invited her to dinner."

"That sounds innocent enough."

"He was a jerk umpteen years ago and he's probably still a jerk." Sarah set down her cup too hard, and then had to wipe up the spilled juice with her napkin. "Most men are."

Lois regarded her younger daughter fondly. "Honey, you're only twenty-nine. That's too young to be so cynical."

"It's not as if Rick was the first creep I ever ran into." Sarah had always tended to fall for guys with commitment issues.

"Experience is a great teacher. You're developing better judgment," Lois said encouragingly.

"Enough judgment to recognize that I'm happiest alone."

Still curious about her friend and mentor, Diane intervened. "You didn't finish telling us about Alice. Is she going to meet this George?"

"She hasn't decided," Lois answered. "For one thing, she claims she's not keen on finding out how her old dreamboat looks at sixty-seven."

"Why not? All those wrinkles ought to kill any lingering romantic regrets," Sarah remarked.

"Perhaps she doesn't want him to see how *she* looks fifty years later," Lois countered. "A lot of us have a hard time believing we're this old. I certainly don't feel like I'm seventy."

"I have the opposite problem. I'm only thirty-three. Some days, I feel about ninety." Perhaps that was why she found the chemistry between her and Josh so appealing, Diane realized with a start.

After Will died, she'd considered the falling-in-love part of her life over forever. After all, she had her daughter and her career. This flirtation—if she could even call it that—at least confirmed that she hadn't entirely lost that part of herself.

A pucker formed on Lois's forehead. "Oh, honey, it's about time you started living again."

"I *am* living," she said automatically.

"Me, too. Now enough with the advice," Sarah commanded. "Back to work."

Still grumbling playfully, the three of them settled in the living room again. The worn couch and overstuffed chairs might never grace a decorating magazine, Diane mused, but they always reminded her of childhood holidays, in the happy years when her father and grandparents had been alive.

Twisting a strand of multihued yarn around her hook, she set to work. Her mother and sister did the same, their mouths identically pursed in concentration.

Fortunately, the three of them all held their yarn with a similar tension, so that their squares ended up the same size. Otherwise, they'd have had a decidedly odd-looking afghan.

"How's the birthday party coming?" Lois asked after a while. "Does Carly like the photography theme?"

"She loves it."

"That reminds me. If you need more entertainment, I could break out my tarot cards. Girls love fortunetellers." While Sarah had never claimed to have any psychic abilities, she was sufficiently intuitive to play the part at parties and fundraising events.

"Thanks, but I'm not sure it's a good idea for this age group. Young girls tend to take these things too seriously. I appreciate the offer, though."

Sarah didn't seem offended. "It was just an idea. Go on. I want to hear what you're planning."

Diane sketched the scenario she and Josh had worked out, complete with pizza and a photo scavenger hunt. When she finished, Sarah probed, "How come you keep referring to Carly's father as Mr. Lorenz?"

She hadn't done so consciously. Was she trying to cover her mixed feelings?

"Because he's just an acquaintance," Diane blurted. "It's not as if we could ever be friends, under the circumstances."

"Yeah, I know how you feel. He showed up next door at the Lesters's house with some workmen while I was gardening." Sarah pulled out an errant stitch. "Over the fence, he noticed me pruning that climbing rose and suggested we install a trellis. It's a good idea, but talking to him, well, the words kind of stuck in my throat."

"Seriously? I thought you two chatted for quite a while," Lois observed. "I half expected you to invite him over for coffee."

Was Sarah drawn to Josh? A chill ran through Diane. "I wouldn't have pegged him as your type."

"He isn't. I can't forgive him for what he did to Will." Sarah's hook moved deftly in and out of the square she was working on. "Can you?"

The question caught Diane off guard. Becoming friendly with the man who'd freed Will's murderer *did* seem disloyal, yet there was so much more to him. "The whole situation still upsets me, but I have to admit he's a terrific dad."

"I strongly disagreed with his decision at the trial, but I'm willing to give him the benefit of the doubt," Lois said quietly. "He seems like a conscientious person."

"Maybe so. I'm trying to be charitable," Sarah conceded. "All the same…"

"Give your sister a break," their mother replied more sharply than usual. "She's been in mourning. Then the first man who stirs her interest at all has the bad grace to be Juror Number Seven."

"All she said was that he's a good father," Sarah retorted. "She couldn't possibly be attracted to him."

Diane stared down at her crocheting, afraid to respond.

"Moving right along," their mother remarked, "what are you getting Carly for her birthday?"

"Oh, my gosh!" For all her concern over a theme and goody bags, Diane had forgotten that important item. "What she really needs is a beauty makeover, but I doubt she'd appreciate the offer."

"I'd be happy to chip in for a new hairstyle." Sarah had recently added warm highlights to her own long brown hair.

"She might be less resistant if you treated her and Brittany at the same time," Lois suggested.

"What a terrific idea. Brittany will love it, too."

"Don't wait. You'll have a hard time booking an appointment, as it is." Lois turned her square and worked another side.

"I'll ask if my hairdresser can take them after school on Friday."

"If she can't, you could try the new stylist. Renée. She did my hair," Sarah said. "Her schedule might not be full."

Diane studied her sister's caramel highlights. The stylist had trimmed Sarah's full bangs at an artful angle as well. "She's good."

"I'll bet she'll bend the girls around her little finger," Sarah added cheerfully. "She's gorgeous *and* she's really personable."

"As long as she tames that thicket of Carly's, I'll be happy." Belatedly, Diane wondered what Josh would think of the scheme. She hoped he'd applaud, but she'd have to clear it with him.

As for their plan to shop this weekend, she decided not to mention that. It wasn't a date, after all.

And as Sarah had observed, she couldn't possibly be attracted to him.

ON SATURDAY, Josh carted his power saw down the slope to demolish Brittany's old playhouse. He had to wait until late morning to avoid disturbing any late-sleeping neighbors, and by then, as often happened during September, the temperature had soared.

His T-shirt stuck to his torso and the noise of the saw enveloped him as he worked. It wasn't until he stopped to carry another pile of firewood down the slope that he glimpsed Diane's face at the kitchen window.

How long had she been watching? In any case, she retreated quickly.

Josh carted the boards across the backyard. He sure was a sweaty mess, he thought when he caught sight of his reflection in the sliding door. Beads of perspiration standing out on his forehead, muscles bulging beneath the load.

In the early days, Tiffany used to exult over his rough-hewn physique, as if getting it on with a construction worker constituted some sort of aphrodisiac. The glamourous woman he'd dated after his divorce, a hairdresser named Renée Trent, had admitted she went for the down-to-earth type, too.

But he wouldn't expect that kind of reaction from a teacher. Yet he could swear she'd been staring at him.

Defiantly, his brain conjured up images of Diane alone in her bedroom. She probably wore delicate pink lingerie that showed off the sweet swell of her breasts. Such a beautiful woman deserved a man who'd take her in his arms and tenderly bring her to ecstasy.

What had gotten into him? Must be the sheer physicality of sweat-inducing labor. And the effects of spending too much time without female companionship.

At the hose bib, Josh squirted water over his head. Nothing beat a cold shower for clearing the brain *and* dealing with perspiration.

About an hour later, he removed the last of the wood, then hurried to clean up properly before his shopping expedition. When he'd mentioned it to Carly a few days earlier, he'd received a distracted, "Sure, Dad." He should have reminded her yesterday, Josh supposed, but he'd forgotten.

That might explain why, when he entered the house, he couldn't find her. She didn't answer his repeated shouts, nor was she sitting at the computer with her earphones plugged in.

What would the Bittners think if the birthday honoree failed to show? Using the last option of the desperate parent, he dialed her cell phone number.

A couple of rings. "Hi, Dad."

Relieved, he asked, "Where are you?"

"At Brittany's, like I told you."

She had? "Good. I'll be there at three."

"Suit yourself."

Kind of a weird response, but that wasn't unusual. In the shower, he let the hot water pour over his sore muscles. Freed of restraint, his mind floated free—and picked up where it had left off earlier, on Diane in a delicate bra and panties.

Her lips parted eagerly. Invitation beckoned in her brown eyes, and there was a hint of innocence that tantalized him.

What had her relationship with her husband been like? Josh wondered. In court, the prosecutor had presented the pair as childhood sweethearts. They'd obviously shared a deep connection, but had her passions ever been fully aroused?

Josh had better be careful. If Diane guessed the direction of his thoughts, she'd slam the door on him, literally and figuratively.

After drying off, he pulled a dark-blue T-shirt over his head. They were merely going to the store, for Pete's sake. Well-chaperoned, too. Nothing to worry about.

Since he planned to drive, Josh backed his truck out of the garage. Across the street, he noticed Oliver on the porch of the Lowder house, talking to someone just out of view. Was that Charley or a client? If there were going to be new neighbors, Josh supposed he'd find out soon enough.

Driving downhill and around the bend, he slowed near number 12, where a couple of little girls played hopscotch on the sidewalk. There seemed to be kids everywhere today, tykes frolicking on lawns, older children riding bikes.

This was, as Oliver had described it, an old-fashioned community. Diane talked about the neighbors—not only her mother and sister but the rest of the Foxes, too—as if they were family. A pleasant notion, perhaps, but disconcerting to Josh. Over the course of his family's many moves, he had found out that close-knit communities might be fine for those who grew up in them but they often closed ranks against outsiders.

Maybe he should have stayed in La Habra, where Carly had at least established a few friendships. However, when this house had come on the market at a bargain-basement price, he couldn't resist the chance to remodel and resell it.

He parked in front of Diane's house—number 1 Harmony Road. Her yard had everything in place—clipped lawn, pruned hedge, and by the sidewalk a tidy bed of petunias. Against the house were splashed the fevered pink blossoms of a bougainvillea.

When Diane answered the door, her cheeks were bright, as if with excitement. From behind her drifted delicious baking scents.

Josh enjoyed the way her blouse clung to the curve of her breasts above a trim waistline. Quickly, he raised the level of his gaze. "Is everybody ready?"

"Actually, no." Diane sighed. "I thought Brittany understood that we had plans. Instead, she and Carly decided to hold their baking and photography session this afternoon."

Not an insurmountable problem. Josh wouldn't mind spending a little extra time in Diane's company. "I didn't know about it, either. Why don't we give them an hour? We can review our plans for the party."

She stepped aside to usher him in. Some of that tempting fragrance came from her, he realized as he moved past. "Brittany's not just baking a few cupcakes. As long as she has a photographer, she's decided to go for broke. She could be at this all day."

"You're kidding." How much baking could one girl do?

"I'll show you." She led him through the living room, a refreshing space dominated by white and light-green fabrics. A leaf-shaped celadon platter adorned the coffee table and a splashy painting of a garden fairly leaped off the wall. In the center of the picture he noticed a partly open gate, its vivid scarlet echoed by heart-shaped cushions on Diane's sofa.

Then they entered the kitchen. Josh broke his stride to stare at a bewildering array of cakes, cookies and candies that seemed to cover every horizontal surface.

Carly peered through her camera at one of the arrangements. "This would look a lot better if we had some backlighting."

"How about a lamp from the living room?" Brittany,

whose nose and cheeks were smudged with flour, fussed with the pastries.

"Go ahead." Carly lifted her head. "I'm going to apply more glycerin. The shine is wearing off already."

"You guys are really into this." Josh was impressed. "You're practically professionals."

"We *are* professionals," Brittany corrected him, dusting off her hands over the sink.

"They'll be at this for hours." Diane shot him a what-can-you-do look. "The easiest thing would be for me to run out and choose some stuff on my own. I don't mind, and you'll have the day free."

Disappointment dimmed Josh's spirits. He'd been looking forward to this excursion more than he'd realized. "Why not reschedule for tomorrow?"

"There's church in the morning and dinner at my mom's in the evening. That only leaves the afternoon for homework," Diane explained. Then, for her daughter's benefit, she added, "I don't see why this session couldn't have waited until after the party."

"Because I want to do it *now*." Brittany swooped past them.

From the living room, Josh heard the clink of a ceramic lamp base against a table. "I'd better help." He got there just as a heavy lamp was swaying in the girl's grasp. "Let me get that."

"Thanks, Mr. Lorenz."

"No problem."

On the return route, the two of them squeezed past Carly. The girl was so absorbed in framing her shot that she didn't even notice she was blocking their path.

"They're obsessed." Diane shook her head. "Seriously, leave the whole thing to me."

"That's too much to ask." *And I don't want to.*

"No, it isn't."

Usually, Josh enjoyed having a few free hours to fool around with the designs for his dream house. Today, however, the idea left him cold.

He'd prefer to spend the afternoon with Diane. Not a date, exactly. Just…getting better acquainted.

Leaving the girls behind might actually be a bonus.

How could he persuade her to let him go along, without making her uneasy about the situation? What he needed was a flash of inspiration.

To his amazement, he got one.

Chapter Seven

The fluorescent lights flickered maddeningly. Struggling to reposition the heavy living-room lamp, Brittany grumbled, "Honestly, Mom, can't you get that fixed?"

"We'll have to turn them off," Carly said. "They're awful."

"It's the ballasts," Josh informed them. "While we're out, Diane and I can swing by a builders'-supply store."

To his ears, he'd dropped the remark with just the right casual note. He tried not to spoil the effect by staring at Diane too eagerly. *Take me with you.*

Diane drummed her fingers on the table. "That's kind of you, but…"

"Mom, stop doing that. You'll make the cheesecake crack."

"Sorry." She stilled. "Honestly, there's no reason for Mr. Lorenz to waste his time."

"It's hardly a waste," Josh persisted. "You're the expert on parties and I'm the expert on home repairs."

"You should both go," Carly announced. "Otherwise, you guys are going to drive us crazy."

"Yeah." Brittany flinched as the overhead lights wavered again. "Mom, you keep saying what a pain these are."

"I can hire a handyman," Diane protested.

"If you insist on repayment, feed us dinner. Looks like there'll be plenty of leftovers." Josh gestured at the baked goods.

"With glycerin sprayed all over them? I don't think so." Finally registering the girls' exasperation, Diane yielded. "We'll pick up fried chicken."

"Yay!" Brittany cheered. "She hardly ever lets me eat fast food."

"We have fried chicken a lot." Carly shot her father a grin, perfectly aware that she'd just embarrassed him.

"We won't be long," Diane said ominously.

"Take hours," Brittany suggested.

Josh tried to smother his laughter as he accompanied Diane out the front. "When did our little girls get so bossy?"

"Brittany was *always* bossy," she responded tartly.

He held the truck door open for her. "Carly was never a terribly compliant child, but when this preadolescent rebellion hit I figured she'd get over it soon enough. Talk about delusional thinking."

Inside the cab, Josh felt Diane's energy surround him. Despite her pulled-together manner, he again sensed something powerful stirring beneath the surface.

Something that had to do with him.

Diane swallowed. "Raising a child alone is tough. How long have you been divorced?"

"Four years. We were separated for a year before that. I'll save you the math—Carly was nearly seven when we split." Josh watched out for children at play, aware that his thoughts easily could be distracted by the vibrant woman beside him.

"It's unusual for a father to get custody of a girl so young," Diane observed.

Why soft-pedal the truth? "Tiffany left me for a rich control-freak investment banker. He didn't like the idea of somebody else's kid hanging around, cramping his style, and she went along with that."

Diane adjusted her seat belt. "Surely she insisted on visitation rights."

"They were supposed to spend this past July together. But they fought so much that after a week my daughter insisted on coming home." Josh had seen relief on his ex-wife's face when he'd arrived to pick up Carly.

"Is that when she started dyeing her hair?" Diane ventured.

"Oh, she got into that *before* she went." Josh smiled. "Sort of a test for her mom, I'm guessing. A deliberate provocation."

"That's a preadolescent girl for you."

He considered pointing out to Diane that *her* daughter didn't seem to act that way. But sweet as she was, Brittany had her sharp side, too.

"Where should we start? The mall?" Josh didn't visit the place often, except for the occasional trip to buy tools at the department store.

"I'd prefer the party store," she said.

"You mean it isn't just one of those tiny boutiques stuck in a corner?" That's what he'd been imagining.

"Are you kidding? It's huge."

"Just point me in the right direction."

"Left at the next light." She settled back with a glow of anticipation.

Josh felt a corresponding thrum. But it had nothing to do with picking out paper plates or party favors.

RIDING BESIDE a man, sharing a personal conversation—such simple interaction, and yet Diane felt as if she was venturing into new territory. This wasn't a date. Why, then, was she so keenly aware of Josh's nearness? Why, this morning, had the sight of him working in the yard drawn her to the window?

Much as she'd loved her husband, he'd never radiated this kind of elemental masculinity. His touch had been gentle and her responses had been pleasant—and predictable. That had suited Diane, who had preferred the safety of living in an ordered world.

But now, as an adult, she no longer looked to a man to keep her safe. To her surprise, she actually enjoyed this sensitivity to Josh. The sight of his hands on the steering wheel made her breasts tighten and the insides of her legs prickle.

She really *must* get a grip.

Once they reached the party store, she let Josh push the cart while she concentrated on tableware and decorations. Or tried to concentrate. But when he leaned beside her to examine the plates and napkins, her neck registered the whisper of his breath. At close range, she could see that he'd shaved recently, and she itched to touch a small patch of stubble he'd missed at the corner of his jaw.

With an effort, Diane pulled her thoughts into line. "I don't see many items that relate to cameras. How about a movie-making theme instead?" She indicated a collection of tableware covered with images of clapboards and Golden Age movie stars.

Josh picked up a package of napkins for inspection. "Carly really enjoys Buster Keaton and Charlie Chaplin comedies. She ought to love this."

Diane hurried to select everything they required, including prizes for contests. As favors, she chose frames in which each girl could display a souvenir picture.

"We can snap them having fun and then print out the best shot for each guest," she explained.

"You're brilliant," Josh answered. "I can't tell you how intimidating I find this whole process."

He didn't look like the kind of guy who'd be intimidated by *anything*. "What did you do for her other birthdays?" Diane loaded items into the cart.

"The La Habra Children's Museum, Chuck E. Cheese, whatever was popular with Carly's friends." Ruefully, he noted, "In those days, she had quite a few friends."

"Some kids are naturally meeters-and-greeters, but that's not so important," Diane assured him. "One or two pals are plenty."

"You think so?"

"How many friends do *you* have?" she queried. "Or does any grown-up?"

"You have the Foxes," he said.

"You're ducking the question."

"There's a couple of guys who drop by to watch ball games. I hang out with Oliver Armstrong occasionally." A touch defensively, he added, "His cousin Rafe is a good guy, too."

Impulsively, Diane asked, "No female friends?"

"Not recently."

Some imp must have seized control of her tongue, because she followed up with the comment, "Carly might benefit from having a stepmother." She nearly choked as she said it. "Theoretically, I mean."

"She liked the lady I was dating about a year ago, but it didn't work out," Josh said tersely.

Diane waited to see if he would say more. He didn't.

Unlike her, he obviously had some experience with dating. Well, she couldn't assume the guy had lived like a hermit since his divorce, could she? All the same, she wondered what sort of woman he usually hung out with, and why he'd broken up with the last one.

Which was absolutely none of her business.

After he paid for their purchases, they walked outside into the rapidly cooling air. In Orange County, temperatures often dropped thirty degrees at night.

"I guess that wraps it up," Diane said. "Let's head for the fried-chicken place."

Josh clicked open the truck. "Aren't you forgetting something?"

"You mean my gift?" What a perfect opportunity to discuss Carly's hair. Perhaps it was a good thing the girls *hadn't* come.

"I meant the home supply store. But if you'd like to stop at a gift shop, that's fine with me."

How accommodating of him. Diane wished the man wasn't beaming at her quite so endearingly as they got into the cab, though. It brought out a boyish charm that made her want to ruffle his hair.

"Actually, I had something else in mind. A new hairstyle," she told him. "For Carly *and* for Brittany. What do you think?"

"I think I'd throw in a length of rope and some handcuffs to drag her to the salon, if necessary."

Diane chuckled. "How to win over a teenage girl!"

Josh eased out of the parking space. "Okay, forget the handcuffs, although we might still need the rope. I'd be happy to spring for a manicure, by the way. That purple polish gives me the creeps."

"My sister and mom want to pitch in on the gift. That'll more than cover a manicure," Diane told him.

"You discussed my daughter with your family?" He sounded surprised.

She hoped she hadn't been tactless. "They've taken an interest in her since she stopped by for tea. We were sitting around crocheting an afghan for the church bazaar, and they asked about the party."

"Crocheting? Sounds cozy." Josh's mouth quirked. "What else did you talk about?"

"What do you mean?"

"My name didn't come up? I'm hurt."

She felt her face grow warm. "Sarah mentioned your suggestion about installing a trellis. That's a good idea. That climber goes all over the place."

"Nothing else? Such as, 'Gee, Josh Lorenz was working in my yard with his shirt off and I couldn't stop staring,'" he pretended to quote.

By now, Diane suspected she must be bright red. "I did *not* stare."

"You're cute when you blush."

She fanned herself with one hand. "It's hot, that's all."

"Not any more." He indicated a temperature reading posted atop a bank sign. "Seventy-nine and dropping."

"Didn't anyone teach you not to contradict a lady?"

"Sorry. I didn't intend to mention the fact that I saw you watching. I was flattered, that's all."

She considered further denials, but why bother? Besides, she'd rather enjoyed the teasing.

At the building-supply store, cars filled the lot. Couples and families with kids pushed shopping carts to their vehicles. A busy day for married folks, Diane reflected with a pang.

She had to stop torturing herself. And get out more. With or without Josh.

From near the front of the store, the sound of guitar music penetrated the hum of motors and the clattering of carts. "Feel free to buy extra stuff while we're here," Josh told her. "The truck has plenty of room."

"Can't think of anything." The house cried out for sprucing up, but Diane's budget could handle only the most urgent items.

When Brittany moved on to high school and no longer required a tuition break at Brea Academy, Diane planned to check out better-paying jobs at public schools. Then, she'd love to indulge in new linoleum and a stovetop with pilot lights that didn't keep going out. Wild and crazy stuff like that.

On the walkway outside the store, they strolled past huge tubs of poppies and snapdragons. Diane was fond of pansies, too, but so were the neighborhood snails, which ate them right down to their roots.

As they neared the entrance, she realized the guitar music wasn't recorded. A raggedy fellow sat on a folding stool, strumming an instrument with eyes half closed. On the ground, an upturned cowboy hat was positioned for donations.

Whenever she and Will had encountered the homeless, he'd always hurried past with a touch of embarrassment, so Diane wasn't prepared for Josh's response. He stopped, waited for the man to finish, then addressed him respectfully. "You're good. Ever play in a band?"

"Used to tour with a group." The guy shifted awkwardly. "Got in a motorcycle crash and scrambled my brains, not to mention my legs."

Josh dropped a twenty-dollar bill in the hat. "I run a couple of construction crews. Do you have any skills in that area?"

"I used to paint houses, but the vertigo's gotten too bad." The man, whose long hair looked cleaner at close range than Diane had assumed it would be, must have noticed her uneasy stance. "Sorry. I know I make some folks uncomfortable."

"I'm the one who should be sorry," she apologized.

"No, you ain't." A grin revealed a gap between his teeth. "I lived hard in my younger days. Was drunk out of my head when my bike crashed. Lucky for me, my parents took me in and their church found me a part-time job, but I still love strummin' this old guitar."

Josh handed the man a business card. "Call me if you get in a bind."

His bright-blue eyes glimmered. "That means a lot, man. Thank you."

Even after she and Josh were inside the warehouse, Diane's thoughts remained with the guitarist. And with Josh's treatment of him.

"You were wonderful to that man," she said. "Most people would ignore him." *Like Will and me.*

Will had done his share of good deeds, though. As a teacher, he had sometimes come home thrilled when a frustrated child finally grasped an elusive math principle. He'd volunteered at a homework help center, as well.

Josh pushed their cart briskly along the aisles. "When he was twelve, my brother Tim was diagnosed with brain cancer. As he got older he moved with a jerky gait, which other kids mocked. Some people gave us a wide berth on the street. I learned not to assume the worst just because someone appears different."

Diane noted the tension in his voice. "Is your brother still alive?"

He shook his head. "He died a few weeks before his eighteenth birthday."

"I'm sorry. That must have been rough on you."

He seemed to gaze beyond their surroundings. "To a kid as young as I was, living with a cancer patient began to seem normal. For a while, I believed we could go on that way indefinitely—my parents running to the hospital, money short, us moving from one apartment to another as the rent increased. The spurts of hope and then the letdowns." He blew out a puff of air. "Hey, what hit me? I didn't mean to spoil the mood."

"I'm glad you told me." Diane appreciated the trust that showed. And the courage. When she met new people, she often let them assume she was divorced just to avoid dredging up painful memories.

"Ah, here we are. Ballasts." After checking the specifications, he transferred a couple of boxes from a shelf to their shopping cart.

"I appreciate your installing them for me." She wasn't even sure what a ballast was.

"You think I'd have survived shopping for Carly's birthday party by myself? I'm getting the best of the bargain."

Although Josh had resumed his easygoing attitude, the subject of his brother's death lingered for Diane. This man had unsuspected depths and a background quite different from hers. No wonder his reactions were so often at odds with hers.

When they went outside again, the guitar player had disappeared. Diane hoped he was enjoying a good dinner with his twenty dollars, which reminded her of the final task on their agenda.

"Fried chicken," she said.

"I'll pay," Josh insisted. "If you can persuade my daughter to do something socially acceptable with her hair, I'll buy you dinner every night for a week."

"Only a week?" she teased. "Just kidding."

"You sure?"

"It's back to balanced meals for us."

She refrained from suggesting that he and Carly might benefit from less fast food, as well. She wasn't about to start running this man's life. They'd already grown closer than she'd intended them to.

After the party, they'd probably see much less of each other. And that, Diane told herself, was probably a good thing.

Chapter Eight

The girls were happily thinking of names for Brittany's cake-baking enterprise when Diane pulled into the Archway Center the following Friday afternoon. Located only a few miles from home, the Hair Apparent Salon lay just past Archway Real Estate and Smile Central in the middle of the shopping strip.

She'd driven them there straight from school. Several other sixth-graders who'd called out "Have a nice weekend!" to Brittany had displayed surprise at seeing Carly with her. That, plus the anticipated improvement in her appearance, ought to boost her status considerably. Or so Diane hoped.

Thank goodness for Brittany's influence. She'd leaped at the prospect of a professional haircut, since Diane usually trimmed her bangs and shoulder-length locks at home. Her eagerness had swept away Carly's initial reluctance.

Diane parked in a space out of sight of the orthodontist's office. Best to avoid Dr. Salonica, whose son had just scored a B-minus on the weekly spelling quiz.

"Baking by Brittany's my favorite." Her daughter examined her notes. "Let Them Eat Cake is cute, but what if a customer threatens to cut off my head?"

"It's your company. You get to pick. Just don't go with Sweet Stuff," Carly shot back. "That's puke worthy."

"I won't. But if you bring up Hottie Treats again, I *will* be sick."

"Okay, girls. Enough references to upchucking." Diane unlocked the doors. "Carly, enjoy your birthday present."

"This'll be fun," Brittany added.

"Only with you," said her new friend.

"Really?"

"I'm a little nervous."

"You'll look great!"

Diane said a silent prayer of thanks. Carly and Brittany had been getting along fairly well since the previous weekend. The adults had returned with a bucket of chicken as the girls finished the photo shoot, and they'd all gathered around the kitchen table. Diane had enjoyed listening to the two girls discuss designing an ad. Carly's skills, she learned, included computer graphics.

"You should volunteer for the school yearbook," she had ventured. "They could use someone with your talent."

"Yeah, seriously," Brittany had agreed.

"Maybe." At least Carly appeared to be giving the idea some consideration.

And she'd agreed to the new hairstyle. Quite a few changes all at once. Diane sympathized, recognizing how hard she herself found leaving the past behind.

Take her own hair. Will had loved her long hair, a style she'd worn since high school. Now, as they entered the salon, Diane glanced at posters of models and debated trying something different.

Not today, though. This visit was for the girls.

Inside, Diane waved to Cheryl, her usual stylist, who'd

been booked solid for today. Cheryl waved back and pointed to another station, mouthing, "That's Renée."

"Wow," Brittany said, eyeing the woman busy styling a customer. "She's gorgeous!"

The new lady had a mane of blond hair, a spectacular figure and large up-tilted eyes set in a sculpted face. How fortunate that she was surrounded by women—in any other setting, she'd have wreaked havoc among the men.

Diane squelched a niggle of insecurity. So what if her figure had a few bulges and her face would never launch a thousand ships? This wasn't a competition.

"Renée!" Carly's delighted cry caught her off guard. "I didn't know you worked here."

They knew each other?

"*You're* the birthday girl?" The blond woman swooped over and wrapped her arms around Carly. "Honey, it's great to see you. I swear, you've grown four inches."

"Three," the girl corrected, beaming.

"Did you used to live in La Habra?" Diane asked, as Renée stepped back.

"Huntington Beach." That was a forty-five minute drive from Brea. "I'm moving to the area." She didn't explain how she knew Carly.

"Thanks for fitting us in." Diane introduced herself and Brittany.

"Just let me finish with this customer, and we'll get started," Renée promised.

"Of course."

The three of them took seats in the waiting area. Although she picked up a magazine, Diane didn't open it. "How do you know her?" she finally asked, unable to contain her curiosity.

"She and Dad used to date."

Suddenly, the room felt much too noisy and crowded. "Oh?"

"His company remodeled the salon where she worked. That's how they met."

Diane tried to remember what Josh had said about his former girlfriend. Only that the relationship had ended. No details. "She seems very nice."

"Yeah. I miss her."

Brittany, who'd been leafing through a hairstyles magazine, broke in. "What about this cut? For me, and maybe you, too."

"Let's see." Carly became absorbed in examining the pictures, her head bent close to her new friend's.

Clutching the magazine in her lap, Diane watched Josh's former girlfriend across the room. A knockout. Had distance been a factor in their breakup? If it had, Renée was a whole lot closer now.

I am not going to obsess about this. For heaven's sake, Josh wasn't dating anyone, including Diane. And if he fell for this stunning goddess, who also came across as a decent person...

Well, Diane was going to care a whole lot more than she wanted to.

AT ELEVEN O'CLOCK Saturday morning, Diane halted her car in front of the Lorenzes' house. Earlier, she'd made half a dozen trips via the hillside steps to decorate, but they'd decided to deliver the baked goods by car.

"Look. They sold Mr. Lowder's house." Her daughter pointed across the street. Sure enough, Oliver Armstrong was affixing a Sold banner on top of the For Sale sign.

"Charley must be relieved. He's eager to join his grandkids." The departure of such a neighborhood old-timer saddened Diane, although she hadn't been close to the man. "I wonder who's moving in?"

"If that's their car, it's cute."

Cute wasn't exactly the right word for the red convertible parked behind Oliver's sedan. *Sexy* sprang to mind. "I can't imagine a family with children driving around in that."

"Maybe they don't have kids."

"Probably not." From the trunk, Diane collected the snacks that Brittany had prepared. Her daughter insisted on being the one to carry the camera-shaped cake.

Cooking and baking went a lot more smoothly when the overhead lights didn't flicker, Diane mused. As did grading homework and reviewing lesson plans. She'd been grateful to Josh all week.

"Mom!" Brit was still studying number 17. "Isn't that Renée?"

The blond woman emerging from the house had her face averted, so all Diane could see were long, slender legs and shorts so tiny they ought to be banned. "I can't tell. Anyway, didn't she say she'd already moved to the area?"

"She might have been renting till now."

Their subject swung toward Oliver, the striking features even more beautiful in daylight than at the salon. It *was* Renée Trent. Josh's ex-girlfriend had moved right across the street from him.

She spotted them and waved. "Hey, I don't believe it! Do you live there?"

She doesn't know. But whatever Renée's motive in buying the house, she was going to be right there in all her radiant glory. While styling the girls' hair, she'd joked about a disastrous date the previous weekend, which meant there wasn't a regular boyfriend in the picture.

Diane ordered herself to rise above her insecurity. And jealousy. "No, we live down the slope. The Lorenzes own this house."

"Really?" Renée asked in surprise. "You mean Josh and Carly?"

"The very same."

Oliver joined the conversation. "You folks know each other? I told you this was a great neighborhood."

"It sure is." Renée indicated the cake in Brittany's hands. "Did you bake that? It's fabulous."

The girl glowed. "Thanks. It's supposed to be a camera."

Squelching her anxiety, Diane somehow got through the next few minutes of chitchat. This might be blessing in disguise, she told herself as she and Brittany went into the house. If she was going to lose a connection with Josh, better that it should happen now, before matters progressed any further between them.

Somehow she failed to find the thought comforting.

JOSH COULDN'T stop marveling as his daughter scurried around checking the camera batteries and wrapping contest prizes. She'd become an organized young woman and a beauty he hardly recognized.

A shining mass of chestnut hair had replaced the old pink-and-purple tangle. Tamed, the natural curls softened the broad contours of her face, and Carly had bypassed her usual Goth clothing in favor of jeans and a blue-and-tan Brea Academy T-shirt.

The manicure hadn't quite gone as Josh had hoped. Instead of a pale-pink shade, Carly had chosen blue-and-white stripes with tiny red stars. Still, they beat the heck out of dark purple.

The only other downside was her endless chatter about Renée Trent. Not that he harbored any ill feelings toward the hairdresser. She was a kindhearted person and ten-car-pileup gorgeous.

During the year they'd dated, however, he'd discovered that

she never truly let anyone close. Their relationship had plateaued and finally they'd parted by mutual consent. He missed her as a friend, but nothing more.

"They're here!" Carly called.

Josh followed her to the door. Diane glowed in a figure-hugging white-and-pink sundress. To his disappointment, she responded to his warm greeting with a stiff smile.

"What's wrong?" he asked after the girls bustled ahead to the kitchen.

"Nothing." She maintained a cautious distance.

Was it possible she suspected his interest and meant to discourage it? In their shared concern about Carly, she'd set aside her initial hostility, but he'd kept expecting it to crop up again. Yet he hadn't notice any tension this morning when they'd been hanging streamers and inflating balloons.

In the kitchen, Diane engaged her daughter in what struck Josh as a pointless series of discussions. Whether to set out the snacks before or after the pizza. Where to display the pile of prizes. Which girls to match in teams for the scavenger hunt.

Again, he sensed she was avoiding him, but couldn't figure out why. Being around women sure could confuse a guy.

Josh turned his attention to replacing a blown light bulb, and then he ordered a stack of pizzas with toppings from a list Diane had prepared. Meanwhile, he picked up a few enlightening details from the stream of conversation.

Renée had bought the house across the street. Oliver should be pleased on many levels, Josh reflected. Renée was exactly his type, and neither of them appeared to want a serious relationship.

The doorbell heralded the arrival of their first guest, Suzy Ching, who lived down the block. Carly's old friends from La Habra arrived a few minutes later. Despite some initial awkwardness, the girls were soon absorbed in discussing their favorite movies, and then the pizza arrived.

Afterward, Diane gave instructions for the photo hunt. Each of the three La Habra girls was paired with a local girl, and they scurried out, each team determined to be the first to complete its list.

Josh brought an armload of used paper plates and plastic cutlery into the kitchen. "You're doing a great job."

"They're delightful. I enjoy this." Diane counted the birthday candles as she arranged them on the cake. A curtain of hair helped her to avoid eye contact, as she'd done since her arrival.

Josh preferred to bring the situation into the open. "Have I put my foot in it somehow?"

"What do you mean?"

"You're acting kind of cold. I thought maybe I'd messed up this morning."

"No, of course not." She wiped her hands on her apron. "Cold—that reminds me… I forgot to buy ice cream."

"Got it." He'd picked up a half gallon of vanilla.

She located a scoop. "Guess we're ready for the next phase."

"No, we aren't." Stepping in front of her, Josh took the scoop from her hand and set it aside.

"Excuse me?" She tilted her face up, but allowed her gaze to slide past his. That bland expression, in contrast to her customary frankness, had to be a cover-up.

Darn it, she was otherwise so open that her present behavior exasperated him. Better to respond with humor than accusation, though. "Is my left ear that fascinating?"

Reluctantly, she looked directly at him. "Yes. No. I mean, it's… Why are we talking about your ear?"

"Because you're staring at it."

"I am not!"

He longed to catch hold of her shoulders, as he sometimes did when Carly grew evasive. If he gazed into Diane's eyes hard enough, surely he'd see the truth. Instead, he simply said, "Spill it. I'm not moving until you do."

She took a deep breath. "I'm sorry. It's just that this situation feels awkward. I mean, Renée's living across the street, and she's so close to Carly. She should be the one helping with the party."

He couldn't imagine why she believed Renée belonged here. "She can spend time with Carly if that suits her. Personally, I have no intention of inviting her over."

"You don't?"

The vulnerability in the question touched him. "You think I'm interested in her?"

She started to deny it, he could tell. Then she said, "She's stunning. And I like her. I don't see why you wouldn't fall at her feet."

"Because when I'm with her, there's no depth. Nothing beneath the surface, at least not between us." Josh wondered if he'd gone too far. With Diane, it might be dangerous to refer to underlying currents, but he had to press on. "Besides, I find you much more beautiful."

"You couldn't possibly," Diane protested. He touched her waist to reassure her, and heard her breath come faster. He was breathing harder, too. "I'm not fishing for compliments. But she looks like a movie star."

He searched for a way to put his impressions into words. "Despite everything you've been through, you've retained such a wonderful innocence. It gives you this spark, this freshness that makes me feel like a different person. Does that make sense? I want to explore the person I become when I'm with you."

"I'm not sure how... Whether..." Despite the half-hearted protest, her lips parted invitingly.

And beneath that innocence, he glimpsed the fire that was yearning to burst free. Unable to resist, he lowered his mouth to hers.

The warmth of her swept through him—he'd been right about the underlying passion. They touched each other eagerly, their tongues meeting as her body nestled into his, arms clinging, soft breasts yielding to his hardness.

When Diane started to pull back, he simply lowered his forehead to hers and stood perfectly still, as if thoughts could pass between them. She rested there, accepting this new stage, this closeness. Neither of them dared push it any further.

Not now. But soon, he thought.

At a scraping noise from the front of the house, they stumbled apart. Fighting the temptation to swear, Josh moaned, "Kids have the world's worst timing."

"Always," Diane agreed.

From the living room, a girl called, "Are we the first?"

"You can't be done yet, Suzy." Diane went to check. "Let's see your camera."

Josh hoped the girls didn't realize they'd interrupted an embrace. To him, it seemed obvious from Diane's mussed hair and dilated pupils, but most kids he knew generally considered adults part of the furniture.

After a beat, he heard, "You have two pictures of a rosebush and no hairbrush."

"It doesn't say hairbrush," Suzy protested. "It says brush. A rosebush is a kind of brush, right?"

"I told you that wouldn't work," complained her partner.

"Sorry. You have to find a hairbrush. And remember, your own house is off-limits," Diane responded.

"Phooey. Okay, we're going!" Footsteps rushed out.

"We should have been more specific," Diane grumbled as she reentered.

"How about recapturing the mood?" he proposed.

She gave a reluctant shake of the head. "This isn't the time or place."

"Okay. So name one."

Her earnest brown eyes pleaded for understanding. "Starting a relationship might not be wise. We're obviously drawn to each other, but…"

"What we need," Josh told her, "is a lot more kissing. That should help us figure out the next step."

"What a nutty idea." She couldn't help smiling, though.

"We'll enjoy the heck out of it, right?" He had to stop then, as a commotion at the front door announced the return of Suzy and her partner, with the other four girls on their heels.

Thank goodness they'd bought rewards for second and third place. Everybody won a prize.

The girls proceeded to shoot photos of themselves clowning around. Diane provided costume props—big hats, a feather boa, a glittering shawl—and makeup. Delighted, the guests trooped upstairs with Carly to print out the best shots for their souvenir frames. Josh couldn't remember the last time he'd seen his daughter bubbling with so much happiness.

He felt pretty happy himself. He and Diane had finally touched each other at a new level. Neither of them could deny that they were becoming more than casual acquaintances.

He should have known this pleasant buzz wouldn't last, however. He'd forgotten that he'd invited his ex-wife, who arrived just as the girls were finishing dessert.

Unfortunately, she wasn't alone.

Chapter Nine

On hearing the doorbell, Diane called, "I'll get it!" One of the moms must have arrived early, she figured. Well, they had plenty of food to share.

Thank goodness the hubbub over the scavenger hunt and the photo shoot had prevented any further close encounters with Josh. She was still struggling to sort out her reaction to their kiss.

For the first time in years, she'd come fully alive. Moreover, the thrilling edge to her response had been new. Not only new between her and Josh, but new entirely.

In high school, she and Will had gradually progressed from stolen kisses to making out. Their first lovemaking, in college, had involved both pleasure and trust. But not such fierce heat, not this inner call to adventure.

Distracted, she opened the door to two flamboyant women. The younger, about Diane's age, was a brunette knockout with an exotic cast to her features. The elder, dramatically tall and heavily made up, must have been striking in her youth. Both wore tight-fitting slacks and wafted clouds of perfume laced with peppermint.

"Can I help you?" Diane asked.

The older woman sniffed. Perhaps she was allergic to all that perfume. "Who are *you?*"

Josh arrived at her side. "The party's nearly over, but if you'd like to give Carly her gift, I'm sure she'll appreciate it."

These must be relatives of the birthday girl. Thank goodness they hadn't barged in sooner and interrupted the fun.

"Who's this woman?" the younger of the pair demanded.

Diane saw Josh flinch at the rudeness. Although he replied calmly, she sensed his irritation. "This is my neighbor, Mrs. Bittner. Her daughter is friends with Carly. Diane, this is my ex-wife, Tiffany, and her mother, Flora."

"Nice to meet you," Diane said, politely if not truthfully.

Neither woman returned the greeting. "Aren't you going to invite us in?" Flora demanded.

Coolly, Josh stepped aside. The women swept past them toward the dining room.

Their entrance squelched the lively conversation. The girls studied them with curiosity, except for Carly, who shifted uneasily in her chair. "Hi, Mom. Grandma."

"Honey!" Roaring forward, Flora bumped into a table and sent punch sloshing. She neither apologized nor offered to clean up.

Carly submitted to an embrace, then rose and approached her mother, who bestowed a small hug.

Flora produced a shiny package from her purse, stumbled and gripped the table for support. She must have been drinking, which accounted for the camouflaging smell of peppermint. "This is for you, sweetie. Go ahead and open it."

Carly took it gingerly. "We'll do the gifts in a few minutes."

"It's *special*," her grandmother insisted.

"All my guests' presents are special."

Brittany broke the silence that ensued. "Please have some

cake." She reached for a pair of clean paper plates. "I baked it myself."

Tiffany, who was so thin she probably hadn't eaten dessert since her own twelfth birthday, cast a longing glance at the dessert. Her mother cut off the subject by declaring, "If you won't open it, I'll do it for you."

Snatching the gift from her granddaughter, Flora ripped the paper. A couple of girls gasped at the sight of a grandmother behaving so badly, and Josh's jaw tightened.

From the package, Flora plucked a tiny string bikini. It barely covered the palm of her hand. "The perfect thing for the California teenager—go ahead. Try it on for your friends."

Carly turned pink. "I'm not a teenager yet, Grandma."

"Close enough!"

Over his daughter's head, Josh's gaze met Diane's. She interpreted that as a plea to intervene before he lost his temper.

"As long as we're opening presents, let's move to the living room," Diane announced. In response to her no-nonsense teaching voice, the girls hurried to comply, with Tiffany and her mother trailing after them.

To Josh, Diane murmured, "Any chance they'll get bored and leave?"

"I'm not taking bets," he growled. "Thank goodness you're here. The sight of me pitching an old lady out the door isn't the kind of birthday memory I'd planned for my daughter."

As they went into the living room together, his hand brushed hers. A glow spread through Diane. How unexpected—and gratifying—to feel like part of a team.

JOSH NEVER underestimated Flora's ability to arouse trouble, which was one of many reasons he didn't try to remove her forcibly from the premises. The former Las Vegas showgirl had an arsenal of tricks, including feigning injury. She'd managed to get her second husband, or perhaps it was her third, arrested and held overnight on one occasion, even though she'd been the one who'd assaulted *him*.

He thanked his stars for Diane's support.

In the living room, tension showed on the girls' faces. Carly, who a short while earlier had been bursting with joy, regarded her gifts as if they were hand grenades.

"Which one's from you, Dad?" she asked.

He pointed. She removed the bow and paper, and beamed at the computer software. "This is perfect. I can design my own photo books."

"When you're ready, you log into a Web site and place your order. The kit includes a gift certificate for a couple of finished albums," Josh told her.

"I love it!" She ran over and hugged him.

With a camera that someone had left on the table, Diane snapped the two of them. Josh, nearly overwhelmed by tenderness, suspected he'd be ordering a blowup of that print.

To Joshua's surprise, he caught the glint of tears in Tiffany's eyes. She did love Carly, he knew. Too bad those moments of maternal tenderness were so rare and fleeting. And that she'd never developed the backbone to stand up to her mother.

"Open mine next!" cried one of Carly's La Habra friends.

"Then mine," another girl urged.

Flora frowned. She hated to be upstaged. "Everyone must be dying to see how you looking in the bathing suit."

Tiffany clamped a hand on her mother's arm. "That's enough."

Amazed, Josh regarded his ex-wife with a touch of new respect. It was short-lived, however.

"Enough of what?" Beneath the makeup, Flora paled. Was that anger—or wooziness?

"I didn't mean anything," Tiffany protested.

"Let go of me!"

Her daughter released her arm. "I'm sorry."

Diane approached them. "Are you ill?" she asked Flora.

"I'm fine."

"She took too much cold medicine." Tiffany's meaningful glance made it clear she was softening the truth.

"That stuff sneaks up on you." Diane retrieved Flora's purse. "She should lie down until it wears off. Perhaps she'd be more comfortable at home."

"Nobody's going home," Flora proclaimed in her loudest voice.

Tiffany spread her hands helplessly.

"Oh, yes, you are." Carly marched over to stand beside Diane. "Please leave, Grandma. I love you, but it's my birthday and you're embarrassing me."

For a moment, neither Flora nor Tiffany had anything to say. Then Flora sputtered, "Wear that bikini. It'll make a woman of you!" and stumbled out the door with her daughter right behind her.

Josh maintained his guard, half expecting Flora to fly back in on her broomstick, until he heard the slam of car doors and the purr of an engine. "Whew."

"You've got guts," Diane informed Carly.

"Yeah, well, I'm the only person here she doesn't dare tick off," was the response. "Thanks for standing up to them."

"I second that," Josh told her. "I wish I'd caught the whole thing on video."

"Don't forget the presents," Brittany called out.

"Oh, right!" Carly hurried back to her post, and the girls

quickly became absorbed. In a low tone, Diane said, "Flora needs help. I don't suppose she'd consider treatment?"

"I suggested it once. She nearly bit my head off."

Josh refocused on the girls as Carly examined a hair ornament. "This'll look fantastic with my new haircut."

"Let's see." Brittany twisted a length of hair above one of Carly's ears and secured it. The sophisticated upsweep emphasized the delicacy of his daughter's features, Josh noted. Guys were going to start falling for her any day now.

She's growing up. That shouldn't be news. He just wasn't prepared for it to happen so soon.

"You look fabulous," one of the girls exclaimed. "Who did your hair?"

"Renée at Hair Apparent."

At the mention of Renée's name, Josh watched for Diane's reaction. She merely smiled.

A short while later, a carpool parent arrived. Giggling and waving, the trio from La Habra departed with party favors and prizes. Suzy had to leave to babysit her brother, and Carly and Brittany raced upstairs to experiment with the new software.

Diane stuffed torn wrapping paper into a trash bag. "Your poor ex-wife. I can't imagine being raised by such a mother."

"I agree. Having her as a mother-in-law was more than enough for me." Josh didn't care to discuss them further. They'd already caused more than their share of unpleasantness. "In case I forgot to mention it, you were great today."

"The important thing is, Carly survived relatively unscathed. Or unscathed by relatives, as the case may be. With that take-charge attitude, she'll be running for office before we know it." She covered a yawn, the involuntary stretch emphasizing lovely curves beneath her sundress. Josh's palms curved as if molding to her figure.

Yeah, as if she'd appreciate you groping her. Cool it, fella.

"I didn't realize I was so worn out," Diane murmured.

"You might try a nap," he said. "Later, we could all go out for dinner."

Her nose wrinkled. "Dinner? After pizza and cake, I'm *way* over my limit. It's salad for the rest of the week."

"Lucky thing the week ends tomorrow," Josh teased, trying to hide his disappointment.

"Salad rations for next week, too."

If they weren't going to dine together, at least her nap could wait a few more minutes. "May I show you something on my computer? It won't take long." Josh rarely mentioned his dream house to anyone, let alone revealed the specifics.

She raised an eyebrow. "That sounds like, 'Come up and see my etchings.'"

He grinned. "With the girls around?"

She smiled back. "Just kidding. Of course I accept."

They passed Carly's bedroom. "Delete that one," Brittany was saying. "It makes me look fat."

"You're not even close."

"I shouldn't have eaten so much cake. Wait, that's a good shot. You should put that in your memory book."

"I'm glad we didn't take any of Grandma," Carly said fiercely. "Not when she's like this."

"Everybody's got weird relatives," Brittany assured her. "My Aunt Melinda rescues animals. She's got a houseful of critters, mostly wild, that she's nursing back to health. Once she had a baby alligator. It's a miracle they don't eat each other."

"That's Will's sister," Diane whispered.

Josh wished his brother had lived long enough to indulge in eccentricities or fall in love or have a family. Since Tiffany was an only child, Carly didn't have any aunts and uncles.

He'd never thought about how much support an extended family could provide for a child. Not until he'd met Diane and seen how close she was to her own mother and sister.

"Can I meet your Aunt Melinda?" his daughter was asking. "I'd love to take photographs."

"She lives in Florida," Brittany answered thoughtfully. "But who knows? Maybe you could go with me some time."

Quietly, Josh and Diane moved on to his office. He drew up a chair for her beside the computer station and clicked into his program, choosing an overall view of his imaginary property. Instead of a plain diagram, into view popped three-dimensional images of a house, a cottage and outbuildings as seen from above.

"This is Casa Lorenz," Josh said, scrolling over the screen so that she could study the compound from a variety of angles. "It's a dream place I'd like to build in the not-too-distant future."

Diane leaned forward, a stray wisp of her hair drifting across Josh's neck. "Is that a ranch?"

"Not quite. I doubt I'll be able to afford more than an acre, but it's enough room to spread our wings." He explained his desire to build a cottage for his parents, a horse enclosure for Carly, a freestanding workshop where he could raise a racket without disturbing neighbors and, of course, a house.

"That's gorgeous," she said when he zeroed in on the Spanish-style hacienda.

"It's going to have a tiled courtyard with a fountain." He showed her more details, explaining how he'd been inspired by pictures of Moorish architecture.

Although Diane responded with suitable praise, her tone grew increasingly distant. Josh attributed that to weariness, until she said, "You described this as a dream place, but it sounds like you're practically ready to build. When you said the not-too-distant future, exactly how far off did you mean?"

"Another year or so, depending on the market and the remodeling timetable," he explained. "I have to renovate this house and sell it. Then I'll need to locate the right property, possibly in San Bernardino County."

"That's a long way from here." Her voice sounded thick. "Would you relocate your business?"

"Perhaps eventually, but people in the construction industry tend to commute long distances. My company has projects as far away as L.A. and Riverside counties," he answered. "I'll keep my home base around here for a while, at least."

"I see." She stared blankly toward the computer.

With sudden insight, Josh saw his project as it must appear to Diane. Perhaps showing her this had been a mistake. Exciting as it might be to him, to her it meant that he and Carly would be leaving in a little while. But in southern California, people moved frequently. You couldn't base your dating choices on the idea that someone had to stay rooted where they were. Couldn't she just let the attraction between them develop on its own terms?

A noise from behind revealed the girls' presence. "What are you guys doing?" Brittany asked.

Carly peeked over his shoulder. "Why are you showing that to Mrs. Bittner?" To her friend, she explained, "It's this place he intends to build out in the boonies. I mean, when he's ready to retire or something."

Josh frowned, confused by her comments. He thought he'd made his plans clear to his daughter. Okay, that had been a while ago—months, perhaps a year—but she'd leaped at the possibility of owning a horse.

"I told you when we bought this house that we might be

moving again when you finish junior high school," he reminded her.

"No, you didn't. You said I'd be attending Brea Academy."

"You are. It ends with eighth grade." Josh hadn't expected opposition. He was doing this as much for Carly as for himself. "Room for a horse, remember? Our own private kingdom. And don't forget, Grandma and Grandpa Lorenz aren't getting any younger."

"Nobody's getting any younger. I hate that expression!" Carly sounded on the verge of a meltdown.

She must be worn out. They'd woken early, the party had absorbed tons of energy, and of course she'd had to deal with Flora's obnoxious conduct. "You're tired. I guess we all are. Nothing's imminent, anyway."

On that note, Diane arose. "We had a lovely day. I'm sorry we can't accept your invitation to dinner, but we'll do that another time."

"He invited us to dinner?" Brittany inquired.

"Yeah, what's with that?" Carly chimed in. "Are you guys dating?"

"Whoa." Diane waved away the suggestion. "We hardly know each other."

"But you were getting there, till Dad dragged out his let's-me-and-him-move-to-the-middle-of-nowhere scenario, huh?" his daughter pressed. "Nice going, Pops."

He hated when she called him that. And he wished he had a rewind button to zip back to the point where he'd offered to show Diane his design. There really hadn't been any hurry to broadcast his plans. Now, however, it was too late to do more than run damage control. "Nobody's dating anybody."

The girls exchanged glances. "We know denial when we hear it," Brittany proclaimed.

Where did kids learn these psychological terms? "You guys jumped to a conclusion," Josh told them.

"No, we didn't. And delete that stupid program," Carly ordered.

He closed it instead, and wondered how in the world he and Diane were going to handle the girls' notions about a romance. While that heated embrace had brought them closer, their relationship remained unexplored. And, given the circumstances under which they'd first met, fragile.

To his relief, Diane fielded the issue deftly. While steering the girls downstairs, she said, "In case you kids are fantasizing about becoming sisters, remember that good friends are just as important."

Sisters? When had that issue arisen? A guy required an interpreter when it came to understanding young girls.

"It's not the same thing. You don't see Nancy Yoshida nearly as much as you see Aunt Sarah," Brittany countered. "She used to be your very best friend in the world."

"That's because she got married and moved to San Diego."

"If Aunt Sarah gets married, we'll still spend Christmas and Thanksgiving with her, won't we?"

"Well, yes." Diane glanced at him helplessly.

"Let's take this one day at a time," Josh proposed. "Why don't we attend next Saturday's potluck together? The girls can enjoy themselves, and I'd appreciate if you could introduce me around."

Everyone approved the idea. That was encouraging, Josh mused as Brittany collected her cake dish and party favors, and they said their farewells.

He regretted that showing Diane his dream plan had upset her. But ever since his childhood experience of moving from apartment to apartment, he'd longed for a retreat that no one could invade, a refuge from the coldness and occasional hostility of society.

Carly would change her mind. He'd planned this for too long to give it up.

Chapter Ten

What had she been thinking? Diane had allowed herself to care about the last man on earth she should trust. She'd acted like a starry-eyed schoolgirl, and all the while he was planning his eventual escape from Harmony Circle.

And now... Now, she missed him.

On Sunday night, she sat with her mother and Alice Watson at a booth in Giuseppe's Taverna, an Italian restaurant just outside their development. They were there for moral support for Alice.

The purple grapes on the dining room mural had faded, and although clean, the red-and-white-checked curtains clearly were survivors of another era. To Diane, the faded ambiance provided a charming reminder of decades past.

She loved Giuseppe's lasagna even more than her sister Sarah's spaghetti, which Brittany was enjoying at home, but she knew she ought to opt for a dinner salad. She postponed ordering anything until George Tyler showed up.

Alice nibbled on a breadstick. "He's late. Maybe he's not coming."

The wall clock showed 6:35 p.m. "He's only five minutes overdue," Lois pointed out.

"He should have left early."

"Maybe he got a ticket," Diane speculated. "The cops crack down hard on Whittier Boulevard."

"If anyone should be punctual, it's an engineer." The usually composed Alice had been stewing about this encounter for hours. Or possibly days.

Diane hoped George would put in an appearance soon. After fifty years, he owed his former fiancée a little closure, which she claimed was the most she hoped for.

Diane scanned the assorted couples and families patronizing the restaurant tonight. No older single male had escaped their radar—as if Alice could possibly have overlooked him.

As the other two women chatted, her thoughts wandered. She'd been trying to sort out her reactions to Josh Lorenz since yesterday. It seemed disloyal to Will's memory to have kissed him. Sarah would think so, she had no doubt.

As if that weren't bad enough, Diane had felt new and enticing sensations, being with Josh. And that struck her as even more of a betrayal of Will.

Yet she didn't want to spend the next fifty years alone, either. If Josh weren't planning to leave Brea, perhaps their friendship could develop slowly, giving everyone time to adjust. Instead, the discovery of his intentions had further complicated her feelings.

Maybe she should call the whole thing off. But what about the girls? They'd seized on the presumed romance with over-the-top enthusiasm.

This afternoon, while Diane was weeding the garden, Carly had arrived in overalls and a T-shirt, eager to help. She'd proved a ready worker and a delightful companion, except for her references to how much she wished her father would try gardening.

Carly's interest had been genuine, however. She'd shown

particular curiosity about long-term planning, and had asked some thoughtful questions about rotating crops to improve the soil. "It's like you're really rooted here, as much as a bush or a tree," she'd said wistfully after Diane explained how she varied what she planted and made notes to refer to in future years.

"You could plant a garden, too. I'll help you," Diane had offered.

"I think I'll wait. I mean, if Dad really goes through with this dreamhouse idea, I guess we'll have plenty of space there. But it wouldn't be the same." She'd only cheered up when Diane pointed out her flourishing crop of late-season cucumbers and offered her one to take home.

As for Brittany, she'd found her recipe for goulash and announced that she planned to fix it for the potluck, in Mr. Lorenz's honor. "He's dying to taste it."

Diane doubted that. Besides, her daughter would be wasting an opportunity. "Shouldn't you bake? It'd be good advertising for your new business."

"I didn't consider that," she admitted.

"When's your ad going to run in the PTA bulletin?" Diane asked, hoping to keep her daughter's attention on baking.

"I changed my mind about the ad. Carly's designing fliers for me instead. They'll be cheaper." Brittany had jumped up. "Hey, I know what. I'll bake *and* make goulash. Excuse me. I'm going up to their house."

Off she'd run. Later, she'd repeated practically word for word Mr. Lorenz's praise of the handouts.

Was there no escaping the man?

Speaking of men, Diane's attention fixed on a tall, distinguished-looking fellow who'd just entered the restaurant. Across the table Alice went rigid.

Must be George.

"He won't recognize me," the former principal said nervously.

"Did you send him a picture?" Lois asked.

"No. If he can't tell who I am, forget it."

Diane was startled to see the anxious young girl surfacing inside her dignified mentor. *Do we ever outgrow our insecurities?*

Any worries proved unfounded. George started toward them with a smile lighting his face. Despite the wrinkles and silver hair, his openness revealed the young person he, too, had once been.

Alice rose and the pair shook hands. George seemed to be drinking her in, scarcely aware that anyone else existed.

As for Alice, she ducked her head in a coy manner that Diane had never seen before. *And I thought I knew her so well!*

Although George acknowledged the introductions politely, his gaze scarcely moved from his old love. The two of them floated across the room to a booth of their own.

"Aren't they cute?" Diane said.

"I remember when Andy and I used to be like that," Lois murmured. "Oh, never mind. You're stewing over something. Out with it."

"What makes you think that?"

"You've hardly said a word since we sat down. And I recognize that faraway stare. What, or should I say *who,* is on your mind?"

Diane supposed she might as well admit the truth. Her mother was obviously close to guessing it, anyway. "Josh kissed me."

Lois blinked. "I see."

"Are you upset?" she asked.

"No. I just don't understand why *you* are," her mother said.

"I'm not upset!"

"You aren't exactly beaming, either."

Diane sighed. "Oh, Mom, it's so confusing. Just when I'm starting to like him, I find out he doesn't plan to stay in this area."

"Hold on." A waitress approached, and they both ordered lasagna and salad. Diane couldn't stick to a diet today.

When the server had gone, Lois said, "Never mind what might or might not happen down the road. Do you think he returns your interest, or is he fooling around?"

Diane recalled Josh's tenderness. "I believe he's sincere. But he had a bad experience with Carly's mother and…well, he strikes me as something of a loner. I can't count on him to be there the way Will always was."

"You mean this cad hasn't proposed yet?" Lois queried with mock dismay. "And you've been getting acquainted for an entire week?"

Diane folded her hands in her lap. "I suppose I do expect too much."

"If you're asking permission to enjoy his company, whether on a temporary *or* a long-term basis, I certainly don't object," her mother said. "And if Sarah tries to project her antagonism onto you, I'll do my best to set her straight."

Diane toyed with her napkin. "I guess the person whose permission would matter most isn't around to give it."

"You're referring to Will?"

"Yes, and don't tell me it's foolish." Diane dug deeper into her emotions. "In a sense, I feel as if I'm still married. I'd never even kissed a man before Will!"

"You hadn't?" After the waitress set down their salads, Lois continued, "I didn't realize you were that inexperienced. I met your father in college, but there'd been a couple of beaux before him."

"Beaux?" Diane teased.

"I'll stick with the old-fashioned term. These days, women say *boyfriend* when they mean their live-in lover. I refuse to put my dates in that category." Her mother took a sip of water. "More to the point, you're a widow, not a wife. I do understand, because I still feel married to your father, but if I met the right man I'd do my best to get over it."

"Why did it have to be Josh Lorenz, of all people?"

"Life just turns out that way sometimes," her mother replied. "Let's get back to this kiss. How *was* the first time with a guy who's not Will?"

Diane couldn't believe her mom was asking that. And yet, she supposed she herself had raised the issue. "Thrilling."

Lois took a deep breath. "*Unusually* thrilling?"

Diane nodded.

"Well, he *is* gorgeous. Surely Will wasn't lacking in that department, though."

Diane bristled. "Mom. We were both young and inexperienced—that's all." She'd found her home in the safety of Will's arms. "You can't compare different men at different periods in your life."

"You've made my point for me." Her mother set down her fork. "Diane, Will was your first love. That makes him unique and irreplaceable. But he was also a human being with flaws just like the rest of us. The fact that you respond differently to a new man doesn't reflect negatively on your husband or on your devotion to him. Don't put that burden on yourself."

"But this particular man…" Diane didn't bother to finish the sentence. "I wish he'd never served on that jury. I can't just overlook it."

"You could forgive him," Lois suggested.

While Diane believed in mercy, she also put great value on loyalty. "I'm not sure I can."

"That's a choice you'll have to make. But perhaps not quite yet."

Their lasagna arrived, and while Alice and George remained deep in conversation at their table, mother and daughter dug into their meal. The conversation moved on to the latest news about the status of Minnie's cottage.

Sherry LaSalle and her fiancé had paid a second visit, this time accompanied by an architect. Which raised the question of whether they were considering expansion, renovation or a complete rebuilding.

Diane wished they'd find a location more suitable to their high-living style. "I can't imagine why they're interested in this neighborhood. Surely they'd prefer a view lot in the hills."

"Oliver's always touting our family atmosphere," her mother commented. "Sherry's still young enough to have kids."

"All the more reason to blend into the neighborhood instead of tearing down a landmark."

"People who are rich, beautiful and well-known tend to assume others ought to change to suit them. Actually, even some people who have none of those qualities make the same assumption." Glancing across the room, Lois frowned. "Oh, dear. I thought they were getting along so well."

Diane swiveled for a better look. Already on her feet, an obviously indignant Alice tossed a bill onto the table and marched back to her friends.

George stared after her with obvious regret. "He'd better not come over here," she muttered as she sat down between Diane and Lois.

"Dare I ask what happened?" Lois ventured.

"I'd rather you didn't."

George paid his bill. En route to the exit, he hesitated and looked as if he might approach, but Alice's fierce expression warned him off.

The other two finished their meal quickly. Alice didn't speak again until they were back outside in the privacy of Lois's car. Then she burst out, "The nerve of that man!"

"He propositioned you?" Lois started the engine. "That *would* be nervy, after all these years."

Diane, who'd taken the rear seat, hoped George wasn't that lacking in finesse. She'd love to see a happy ending to this interrupted romance.

"No. Actually, *that* might have been interesting." Alice sniffed. "The old fool believes I've been pining for him all these years—that that's why I never married. As if I'm some pathetic old spinster and he did me a favor by contacting me."

Lois steered toward home. "How ridiculous. You never even told your best friends about him."

"Not only that, but after he left, I dated another man for quite a while. It didn't last, which was fine. I enjoy living independently." Her temper flared again. "If George contacted me out of pity or guilt, he can go whistle!"

Diane sympathized. "You must be disappointed. He's the one who initiated contact. Anyone would assume he's missed *you.*"

"That's true," Alice agreed. "I even thought perhaps he regretted throwing away what we had all those years ago. And I *did* enjoy chatting with him at first. But now...he can take his ego right back to Whittier and keep it there."

"If he doesn't see what an accomplished person you are, George must be the most unperceptive person on the planet," Diane said.

"You got that right." Alice scowled. "Now I've got to face

the rest of the Foxes and rehash the whole sorry mess. I wish I'd never mentioned it."

Diane scarcely noted her mother's soothing reply. Alice's remark reminded her that the following weekend's community potluck wasn't simply a casual gathering. It was going to be a hotbed of gossip.

What would people say when she and Brittany showed up with Josh and Carly? There'd be tongues wagging about how the widow in number 1 was interested in the new owner of number 18. Well, she *was* interested, but perhaps she shouldn't be.

For once, she almost wished she didn't live in a place where people took such an intense interest in their neighbors' lives.

HAD DIANE not accompanied him, Josh would have skipped the event at the community clubhouse. Too many inquisitive strangers. Too many staring eyes and straining ears.

On the other hand, for Carly's sake, he appreciated the chance to participate. The entire previous week, the girls had practically vibrated with excitement. They traipsed up and down to each other's houses, conferring repeatedly about Baking by Brittany and debating every detail of the promotional flier.

Located on Fellowship Lane, the clubhouse served several hundred residents. By twelve-thirty, when the Bittners and Lorenzes arrived, the main room and the pool were jammed with people.

Women in skimpy swimsuits paraded in and out, but none of them stirred Josh's interest. He preferred Diane's subtle curves, set off today by a navy skirt and print blouse.

Inside the clubhouse, the clatter of serving dishes and the hum of voices surrounded them. Brittany set her aromatic goulash casserole on the table of main dishes while Carly stacked fliers beside a pyramid of her friend's pastries. The two drifted to the pool area to distribute more advertisements.

"Do you know most of these people?" Josh asked Diane.

"About half. I'll introduce you."

"That's not necessary."

"Here's Alice. You have to meet *her.*"

Alice Watson, a retired principal who served on the homeowners' association board, turned out to live next door to Diane. Next Josh met a retired aerospace engineer named Carson Ingalls, who chaired the board, as well as several other community leaders.

Since many of these people might be potential clients or referrals, Josh did his best to remember their names. He exchanged greetings with Oliver's cousin, Rafe Montoya, and spoke with the boisterous Lesters, whose home he'd just repaired. After filling their plates, he and Diane headed for an empty picnic table on the terrace.

Josh seized the opportunity to speak privately. "Is my daughter fitting in any better at school?"

Sunlight highlighted a couple of freckles he hadn't noticed before. "She didn't tell you?"

"Tell me what?"

"She joined the yearbook staff." Diane's eyes shone with approval. "The other kids appreciate her skill with a camera, now that she's stopped using it as a shield. She's actually in demand for special events."

"I can't believe she's changed so fast." Carly's transformation had been gratifying, although he feared she might still backslide. No use worrying about that now, however. "You and your daughter had a lot to do with it."

"The satisfaction's mutual," Diane replied. "I'm glad they

both get along with Suzy, too. Girls can get jealous in situations involving a new friend."

Josh hadn't considered that. Heck, the whole business of social interaction tended to baffle him, which was why he'd sometimes found it so difficult to help Carly.

Oliver sauntered up, looking every inch the real-estate professional in slacks and a polo shirt. "Hope you don't mind company. The other tables are full."

"You mean we weren't your first choice?" Josh needled.

"Not unless you're planning to buy or sell a house this year. But I don't suppose I have to work *all* the time."

Josh hadn't noticed his friend's companion until the couple sat down. Renée Trent looked spectacular, as always, and bubbled with good spirits.

Josh glanced at Diane. She welcomed the pair openly, and he gathered he'd calmed any concerns she'd had about their new neighbor. The fact that Renée and Oliver seemed on chummy terms didn't hurt, either.

She already loved living on Harmony Circle, Renée told them as she ate. "I never expected it to be such a hotbed of controversy, though."

Diane frowned. "Controversy?"

"I'm afraid I've landed in a little hot water." Oliver glanced around. "Maybe you heard about it."

Josh hadn't. "For what?"

"My guests today. I invited a couple of prospective homeowners. Apparently that wasn't the smartest idea."

Josh had trouble believing the residents were that petty. "You're in trouble for bringing people who don't live here yet?"

"The problem is these particular people," Renée explained. "I'm not sure why. They seem nice enough to me."

Diane pointed toward the clubhouse, where a suave-looking

man with a petite blonde at his side was addressing the board chairman. "You brought Sherry LaSalle and what's-his-name?"

"Winston Grooms *III*," Oliver replied. "Why not? They wanted to talk to other homeowners and explain their plans informally. I figured they'd be doing everyone a favor, bringing this out in the open."

"Bringing what out in the open?" Renée asked.

Oliver filled them in. The gossip, it seemed, was true. The couple did intend to level Freda Fuerte's cottage and replace it with a four-thousand-square-foot house, nearly twice as large as the biggest existing house in the development.

Josh cringed at the thought of the cottage's destruction. He'd prefer to see the charming old place restored to its former beauty. Still, if this couple bought it, they had a right to tear it down and start over if they chose.

Carly and Brittany raced up and squeezed onto the picnic benches. As they ate, they pelted Renée and Oliver with stories about Carly's birthday party and the compliments on her new hairstyle. Brittany handed them fliers.

"Did you bake these?" Renée indicated the apple turnover she'd been nibbling on.

"That's one of my specialties."

"I'd like to place an order right now."

"Wow!" Brittany whipped out a pocket organizer. The girl came prepared. "What do you want to order?"

"Oliver's lending me and my girlfriends his cottage in Oceanside for a beach weekend. I'd like to take along a dozen of these. Can you have them ready Saturday night? We're leaving right after the salon closes."

"Absolutely. I'll throw in some free samples of other pastries, too. It'll be good for business."

"Sharp kid," Oliver observed.

"Thanks." Brittany beamed.

Josh spotted a knot of people gathering around Winston and Sherry. "What's going on?"

Oliver peered toward them. "Oh, for Pete's sake. Don't tell me he's making a presentation. I'd better check this out." Oliver got to his feet. After excusing themselves from the girls, Josh and the women also went along.

Winston Grooms *III*, his jowls a bit more prominent than they usually were in his newspaper photos, had opened a laptop computer and angled it toward the gathering. As the financial-consultant-turned-developer clicked through the pictures, his voice carried over the shouts and laughter from the pool.

"My Caribbean resort is setting a new standard for luxury. We're already booked for the first year and half after the projected opening." Catching sight of Oliver, he added, "This isn't a sales pitch—in fact, it's almost fully funded. I only wanted you to see the architect's talent before I show you what he's going to design right here in Harmony Circle."

"We like Harmony Circle the way it is," one woman commented.

"I can't imagine a better place to live," Winston concurred. "However, I think you'll agree that upgrading is inevitable, and we intend to do it right."

"Inevitable? In whose opinion?" challenged Rafe Montoya. Oliver's cousin, who'd been quite affable when they attended a baseball game, glared as if barely able to contain his rage.

"People are always suspicious of change. You'll get over it," Winston said patronizingly.

Much as Josh found himself disliking the fellow, he felt kind of sorry for Sherry. In person, the much-gossiped-about divorcée seemed smaller and younger than he'd expected, and she appeared to be baffled by the furious looks Rafe was casting them.

Her companion displayed a sketch of a three-story English-style manor, with castlelike turrets and a pillared entryway. "Isn't that a beauty? Believe me, this is going to be a showplace. You'll be bragging about it to your friends."

"I live right across the street and I won't be bragging about it to anyone, you pompous idiot!" Rafe stormed. "We have height limitations in this area, and that's a beautiful old cottage you're planning to tear down. I, for one, refuse to let you destroy our neighborhood."

Beneath her tan, Sherry paled. To Josh, her shocked expression brought back an ugly incident from his youth.

His dad had been arrested—wrongly—on suspicion of stealing plumbing supplies from a house where he'd done a handyman job. Neighbors who'd watched him march off in handcuffs had immediately shunned the family. Kids who'd played with Josh had called him names at school, and one woman had insulted his mother at the supermarket. His mom had hurried off, head lowered, he remembered, wearing a bewildered expression much like Sherry's. Even a family that his folks had considered good friends had turned a cold shoulder, unwilling to risk standing up to the crowd.

A few days later, the police had learned the truth: The homeowner's son had sold the plumbing supplies for drug money. Despite his dad's exoneration, however, no one came by to apologize. As for the former friends, they might have repaired the breach had they tried. But they didn't.

Josh hated seeing that kind of callousness visited on anyone. While the Harmony Circle residents had legitimate concerns, he didn't like this aggressive finger-pointing.

Oliver waded into the fray. "Folks, this is Minnie Ortiz's

decision. As executrix of her sister's estate, she can sell the property to whomever she pleases."

"No one's criticizing Minnie," responded a woman Josh didn't recognize. "But the homeowners' board may have plenty to say about anything that violates the traditions of Harmony Circle."

A chorus of voices rose in agreement. Disgusted, Rafe flung his half-filled soda can into a trash receptacle, where it landed with a thunk.

Oliver shot Josh a pleading glance. The Realtor needed support and, besides, these newcomers had a reasonable point of view.

"I'd much prefer to see someone restore the cottage rather than tear it down." Josh was surprised at how clearly his voice cut through the grumbling. "But private property is private property, right?"

Oliver gave a subtle nod of thanks. Winston smirked, which was annoying. On all the other faces in front of him, Josh read stony disagreement.

From the pool, the lifeguard aimed a megaphone toward them. "The children's swimming competition is about to begin. Would kids age four to six please assemble?"

With a bit of muttering, the homeowners dispersed. Winston shut his laptop, shook hands with Oliver and, to his fiancée's obvious relief, prepared to depart.

Josh caught up with Diane as she returned to their table. "I'm sorry, but I had to say what I believe."

"It's easy for you. You're only here for a year or so, and then you'll move on. But the rest of us will have to look at that atrocity for the rest of our lives."

He couldn't deny her point. "That's true."

Furiously, she tossed a couple of paper plates into a receptacle. "I'm not in a party mood any more. Brit, you can stay longer if you want."

"I'm done." Abashed, her daughter trailed her across the terrace. Josh would have apologized again, but that might only worsen the damage.

Him and his big mouth. Him and his against-the-grain opinions.

Josh hoped the snobbish Winston would turn his attention to another property. Maybe, given a week or so, the whole incident would blow over.

He certainly didn't want to remain on the opposite side of a battle from Diane.

Chapter Eleven

Usually Diane looked forward to the Foxes' monthly dinners. But on the next occasion, a Sunday in October two weeks after the potluck, she found herself dreading it.

She didn't want to discuss Josh Lorenz. How awkward if anyone who'd seen them at the potluck—and quite a few had—assumed they were dating. Far from it! She was so upset after the scene with Sherry and Winston that she'd been avoiding Josh ever since.

Twice, when he'd suggested get-togethers, she'd made excuses. Although he'd appeared disappointed, he'd made both of their lives—and their daughters' lives—miserable by refusing to back down. He must be the most stubborn man on ten continents, or however many continents there were, she thought.

The tension was obviously affecting Carly. She'd resumed annoying her fellow students by snapping impromptu photos and had begun sporting tight-fitting, low-cut outfits provided—according to Brittany—by Carly's mother and grandmother.

Concerned, Diane debated going to Josh's house to make peace. What stopped her was the memory of a solitary figure strolling along the courthouse corridor after the trial. While the other jurors gathered around her, finally free to express their sympathy, Josh had walked away alone, pigheaded and obstinate.

He hadn't changed. If so, surely he'd have come to see *her* and apologize for spouting off about a neighborhood dispute that didn't concern him. For heaven's sake, Diane had grown up in Harmony Circle. She loved this place and its historic cottages. How easy for him to blather away about property rights, when to him this was nothing more than a way station.

Lois had suggested forgiveness, but how many times and under how many circumstances was Diane supposed to let matters ride? She and Josh were obviously incompatible.

All the same, she missed him.

She felt especially bad that the tension between the girls seemed, if anything, to be increasing. Yesterday, while baking at Diane's house, they'd quarreled about how to divide the proceeds from new orders. Carly had demanded a full third, even though Brittany was paying for the ingredients and had assembled and tested the recipes. When Suzy tried to mediate, Carly had accused the other two of conspiring and left in a huff.

Brittany had spent the rest of Saturday alternating between crying spells and gripe sessions.

Diane almost wished the Lorenzes had never moved into number 18. Yet she couldn't forget the excitement she'd felt in Josh's arms. She hurt whenever she thought about him, which she did far too often.

Sunday evening at Alice's house, she was so distracted she barely registered the Foxes' conversation until after dinner, when they were all sitting around the living room.

At last the name *George* penetrated Diane's musings. "He claims that I misunderstood his meaning—that he simply regrets having disappointed me and wondered why I'd never married," Alice said.

"Do you believe him?" Lois asked.

"I *want* to," their hostess conceded. "He's been urging me to go square dancing. I *would* like to learn how."

"So go, already," Lois told her. "You don't have to sleep with the man."

Minnie looked shocked.

"Or worry about getting pregnant if you do," Tess interjected mischievously.

Jane McKay laced her fingers, looking every inch the wise physician. "While we're on the subject, don't assume that a man of his age is free of communicable diseases. If you decide to get intimate, you should take precautions."

"Nobody's sleeping with anybody!" Alice smacked the arm of her chair. "I'll figure this out for myself, thank you all."

"You brought it up," Lois pointed out.

"Well, I'm withdrawing the topic from consideration. Somebody bring up another subject, fast."

Sarah smiled. "We could always swap jokes from the Internet."

"I don't have a computer," Minnie complained.

"All the more reason for us to share."

"Did you hear about the tire store that advertised an end-of-summer blowout sale?" someone asked.

"How about the lawyer who went to court naked? He forgot his briefs," contributed Tess.

Amid chuckles and groans, the gathering broke up. No one had mentioned Josh, Diane observed with relief.

Clutching her empty salad bowl, she hurried outside ahead of her mother and sister. She wasn't in the mood to chat with them.

Footsteps echoed on the sidewalk behind her. She turned just as Renée caught up to her, carrying a covered dish. "I'm parked here," she noted. "I didn't want to carry hot food all the way from my house."

The distance around the horseshoe bend was less than a quarter of a mile, but southern Californians drove almost everywhere. Besides, Renée wore high heels, and the sidewalk *did* slope.

The hairdresser must have noticed her glancing at the shoes. "I'm afraid I'm overdressed. Most of the Foxes wear pants, I see."

"Not me." Diane had chosen a denim skirt. "Guess we're both old-fashioned."

"Thanks for inviting me. Alice said you're the one who suggested my name." Renée stopped beside a sporty compact. "Listen, I don't want to pry, but I'm concerned about Carly."

Diane fought down her uneasiness at the implication that Renée had once again become part of Josh's and Carly's lives. Surely she didn't still feel that ridiculous jealousy. "Has she talked to you?"

"Oliver suggested I consult Josh about remodeling my house, which needs a lot of upgrading," Renée explained. "While he was over, he mentioned she's having problems at school again. And those clothes she's starting wearing! I wince every time I see her."

Renée's friendly concern erased the last bit of Diane's envy. "She might be reacting to our quarrel over his stand on the cottage."

"I was surprised he spoke up."

"He's unbelievably hardheaded."

Renée cradled her casserole. "Has he told you much about his upbringing?"

"About his brother having cancer, and the impact on his family? Yes."

"They were pretty isolated." If Renée felt awkward carrying on a discussion out here beneath a streetlight, she didn't show it. "I met his parents once, while they were visiting. His mom regrets that Josh grew up with a back-against-the-wall mentality, always an outsider, often defending his brother."

Always an outsider. Which is exactly what I accused him of being, isn't it? "Carly must have picked up on that. The way she's behaving, it's as if she's daring people to reject her."

Of course Diane loved Harmony Circle, which was her home. But she hadn't given any thought to how differently Josh must have viewed that angry crowd scene at the pool. Perhaps Sherry and her pompous fiancé had struck Josh as underdogs.

A twinge of guilt ran through her. Perhaps she'd been too quick to judge. At the very least, she should have considered how Carly might feel on overhearing their argument.

"Is there anything I can do?" Renée asked. "I'm very fond of that girl."

So was Diane. And not only of Carly. "Unfortunately, she and Brittany quarreled recently. I doubt I'll have much contact with her outside of school."

"Then you and Josh aren't dating? I'm sorry. It's none of my business, but you were obviously good for him." Renée opened her car door and set the casserole inside.

The observation startled Diane. "You think so?"

"He's got a talent for pushing people away. I hope you can help him break through that."

After bidding her a thoughtful farewell, Diane carried the salad bowl into the house. She visualized Josh's wistful expression the last time she'd declined his offer to take her and Brit to dinner.

He and his daughter were both hurting. He'd tried to mend the gap, Diane supposed. In retrospect, she wished she hadn't been so stiff-necked, but she'd never before had to deal with this kind of conflict in a close relationship. She and Will had been in synch on almost everything.

Maybe that was why she found Josh both more stimulating and more frustrating. Surely she could meet him halfway…? If she could only figure out how.

CHECKING OUT Carly's Web site on Sunday night, Josh kept returning to the photo of Diane that Carly had snapped the day the tree fell into her yard. He knew her well enough now to recognize the defensiveness in her eyes. He hadn't just knocked down her playhouse; by barging into her life, he'd completely thrown her for a loop.

And yet, despite their differences and the resistance on both sides, something special had begun to grow between them. He longed for her companionship in a way that was new to him.

Tiffany had never been the sort of friend he could bounce ideas off, the kind of person he counted on to share his concerns and enthusiasms. After she'd left, there'd been lonely nights, for sure, but he hadn't felt as if he'd lost his best friend.

Most urgently, he needed to talk to Diane about Carly. She was the only person who truly understood his concerns about his daughter.

Almost overnight, Carly had stopped behaving like a young girl. Her rebellion was taking a new and particularly worrisome turn. Doggone Tiffany for purchasing those tight jeans and sweaters, even if, as Carly insisted, she was the one who'd picked them out. They made her look much too grown up for a twelve-year-old girl.

When she'd tossed her old thrift store garments into the trash last week, he'd actually been tempted to snatch them back. Who would have believed that?

Josh moved on through the online photos. Plenty of images of Brittany and Suzy, and pictures from school. Then someone new leaped out at him—a boy showing off on a skateboard and grinning at the camera.

At Carly.

The pictures had been shot here in Harmony Circle, judging by the houses in the background. Who was this guy?

Calm down, Dad. Probably just someone his daughter had run across during a walk. At a guess, he might be high-school age. Too old to take an interest in a sixth-grader, anyway.

Outside his office, Josh heard Carly mounting the stairs. These past two weeks, she'd been a mass of contradictions. Hiding behind her camera, defiantly flashing those seductive clothes and then retreating to her room to sulk. Yesterday, she'd come stomping home, swearing she never wanted to see Brittany again. When he'd asked what was wrong, she'd yelled at him to leave her alone.

Josh closed the browser and opened the program containing plans for his dreamhouse. Generally, working on the project was a welcome escape, but today he couldn't focus on designing a gazebo around the spa or a shelter for Carly's horse. Come to think of it, a year had passed since the closing of the stable where she'd taken riding lessons, and she'd long ago quit bugging him to find a new one. He couldn't recall the last time she'd mentioned horses.

Kids change. Who knows what she wants now?

He went to Carly's room and knocked before entering. She was uploading images from her camera.

"What did you shoot? Anything interesting?" With luck, maybe he'd find out the boy's name.

"Just stuff." She didn't try to hide the screen, though.

Picture after picture showed the cottages that sat below the curve of Harmony Road. She'd captured handcrafted shutters, willow porch furniture and old-fashioned rosebushes. There was a lively image of Minnie Ortiz wearing a sunhat and picking a bouquet, and then the scene shifted indoors to a sunny parlor filled with mementoes. A silver tea set, a polished teak box, an angel figurine.

"Mrs. Ortiz invited you inside?"

"She told me about her sister, how they met their husbands during the Second World War." Carly deleted a couple of poorly lit shots. "They bought cottages next to each other because they were so lonely waiting for the men to come home."

More images scrolled into view. They included a tabletop display of sepia photographs, including a shot of two men in uniform and a pair of women who must be younger versions of Minnie and her sister.

"Freda's husband died in the Battle of the Bulge," Carly related. "She never remarried or had kids. Minnie's family was her family, too."

"You like Harmony Circle, don't you?" Josh asked.

Carly's mouth pinched. She'd applied lipstick with a heavy hand, and her tank top emphasized her budding figure. Josh forced himself to ignore those details. He'd only spark a dispute if he mentioned them.

"I like *parts* of it," she said.

"What was the fight with Brittany about?"

Her chin jutted. "She's being greedy about the baking money. I did a lot more than Suzy, designing the fliers and everything, but Brittany wants to pay us the same. And she's keeping more for herself."

"Brittany's paying you?" That was news to him. "I thought this was *her* business."

"It belongs to all of us!" Without giving him a chance to sort out the issues, she hurtled onward. "They're ganging up on me. I'm the outsider and they're the ones who belong. They're just mean."

Josh had trouble believing that. "Did they call you names? Make snide comments?"

"Not exactly."

"Then what gave you the impression they were ganging up?"

"They just were."

"Because Brittany won't pay you more than Suzy?" he hazarded.

"And when I objected, they *looked* at each other as if they were thinking the same thing. I can't describe it. It's... They're the ones who are friends. I'll never fit in!"

"You're the new kid. Give them a chance."

Agitated, Carly clicked shut the photo folder. "Dad, I have homework. And you can bet Suzy and Brittany are doing theirs *together.*"

He ached for his daughter. Didn't she realize friendships took time to establish? You couldn't expect to fit yourself into ongoing relationships with a snap of the fingers.

He was especially troubled by her insistence that they were ganging up on her. Had he planted that notion in her mind, with his own reaction at the potluck? Josh didn't want his attitude to predispose his daughter to the possibility of rejection.

He needed Diane's input more than ever. Whatever the disagreement between the two adults, they couldn't let it affect their daughters.

She'd rebuffed his last few efforts at casual outings, though. He'd prefer to come up with a proposal she couldn't resist.

How on earth was he going to do that?

Josh mulled over the subject while paying his bills. No inspiration there. A little TV viewing didn't help, either.

Close to bedtime, Carly marched in clutching a bundle of tangled string. *"This,"* she announced, "has to go."

It flew through the air in the direction of the trashcan. As it soared past, Josh recognized Flora's string bikini. Thank goodness his child didn't intend to parade around in *that*. "I'll buy you a new one. You should have a swimsuit."

"Oh, Mom already did. Even *she* figured out how disgusting *that* is." Carly's nose wrinkled.

Whatever style she'd chosen, it would have to be an improvement. "Too bad you won't have a chance to use it much now that summer's over."

"Haven't you listened to a weather report? It's supposed to be in the nineties next weekend. Maybe I can get Renée to take me to the pool."

She sauntered off before he could point out that Renée saw clients on Saturdays. Besides, how much more fun it would be for Carly to swim with a friend her own age.

And that was when the idea struck. At first, it seemed far-fetched. Then, delightfully dangerous.

Josh could hardly wait to put it into action.

Chapter Twelve

On Monday, Dr. Salonica arrived just as school was letting out. He had another bone to pick with Diane, or in this case an entire skeleton.

His son's grades had continued to drag, dipping into the C range with a recent quiz. In addition, last Friday, Nick Jr. had gotten into a playground fight.

"He never had a problem before this year," the orthodontist said. "I think he should transfer to the other fourth-grade class."

Diane believed the problem deserved probing rather than a quick and at best temporary fix. "I'll be happy to support your request. However, I think something deeper is bothering your son. His behavior strikes me as acting out."

She'd been seeing a lot of that, Diane reflected. Today, Carly Lorenz's camera had been confiscated for misuse, and Dr. Kenton would probably ask her not to bring it back for the rest of the semester.

"Acting out? What do you mean?" the father asked.

"Kids often displace their anger by misbehaving in a different context. For instance, a child who's being bullied at school might take it out on a younger sibling at home," Diane explained.

"Someone's bullying my son?"

Oh, dear, she hadn't meant to imply *that.* "Not as far as I've seen. It was just an example. Nick could be distressed by something in his neighborhood or at home. A grandparent's illness or tensions in the family can all trigger inappropriate behavior. Have you been extra busy at work? He might be seeking attention."

"I *have* been putting in long hours," the orthodontist conceded.

"Kids really need their fathers." Brittany certainly longed for hers, Diane knew. "Since my husband died, my mother and I have tried to keep him a part of my daughter's life. We watch videos of them together and remind her of how proud he was of her. It does help."

Dr. Salonica frowned. "I take Nick Jr. to soccer practice and help with his homework as much as most fathers do. I don't see how that can be the problem. But I *am* sorry about your husband."

"Thank you."

Afterward, Diane sought out the principal, who she felt sure would want to know about a parent's unhappiness. At least, the orthodontist hadn't complained to her, nor had he requested a classroom change.

"If your remark hit a nerve, it might serve as a wakeup call," Dr. Kenton advised. "Let's wait and see what happens."

Good advice, but the situation left Diane edgy. After dinner, while Brittany was reading, she went next door to consult her mentor.

The longtime principal of Brea Academy agreed with her successor's views. "I've known the Salonicas for ages. When their daughter Lani was in third or fourth grade, they separated for a few months, and she got so upset she gnawed her fingernails to the quick."

The mention of family tensions might have hit close to the target. "If that's what's going on, I hope he and his wife are willing to do whatever it takes to save their marriage."

"Assuming it's worth saving," Alice said tartly.

"Surely they've built up a wealth of shared experiences. And they have children!" Slipping off her shoes, Diane stretched her legs along the couch. "A marriage is too important to throw away."

"What if they accumulated a pile of shared misery?" Alice inquired. "Not everyone's as compatible as you and Will were."

She had a point. "After we celebrated our tenth anniversary, I used to believe I was an expert on marriage," Diane said ruefully. "It never occurred to me that I'd just been lucky."

"Luck isn't the whole story. There's also maturity." Alice tilted back her recliner.

"And compatibility," Diane pointed out. "We rarely disagreed on anything. When we did, I usually let Will prevail. The few times I felt strongly, he backed off. Neither of us minded."

"So you never enjoyed a good knock-down, drag-out fight?"

Her attitude surprised Diane. "How can a fight be good?"

"Clears the air," Alice said. "Forces you to communicate. If it's the right kind of fight and not the ugly sort where people insult each other." With a twinkle, she added, "I may not have been married, but I *did* see a man for several years."

Impressed by Alice's perceptiveness, Diane decided to risk discussing her conflict with Josh. "Speaking of relationships…"

Unexpectedly, the older woman snapped her recliner upright. "Don't you dare start!"

"What?"

"I'm sorry I ever told anyone about George."

Diane realized that when she mentioned relationships,

Alice assumed she'd been attempting to pry or give advice. "I didn't mean you."

"Oh. Sorry." The doorbell rang. "Excuse me." Her hostess went to answer.

Alice's "Oh, George... I wasn't expecting you," clarified the identity of the visitor. A murmured exchange followed.

Unlikely that Diane and Alice would have a chance to continue their discussion. Perhaps bringing up Josh wouldn't have been such a good idea, anyway.

Diane headed out. In the front hall, George greeted her politely. Despite his dignified stance, the way he shifted about revealed a trace of nerves.

"Good luck," Diane told Alice. "I'll see you later."

"Of course." Her old friend scarcely removed her gaze from George's face.

At home, the scents of vanilla and cinnamon welcomed her. Before she could settle into a task, however, Diane heard Brittany talking to someone in the back of the house.

A male visitor?

She hurried to the family room. Brittany, a novel resting in her lap, sat in her favorite armchair talking to Josh Lorenz.

A surge of pleasure jolted Diane. He looked so appealing, with his open-collared shirt and end-of-day stubble, that she had to fight the urge to hurry over and touch him.

From where he stood, his gaze fixed on her hungrily. "Good, you're here. Not that I wasn't enjoying your daughter's intelligent company."

With an effort, she remained on the far side of the room. "What's up?"

"We were discussing how to fix the situation with Carly. She's out of control, you know." Brittany sounded absurdly precocious.

"When did you earn your degree in psychology?" Diane teased. Without thinking, she exchanged a smile with Josh.

"Mom!" Her daughter shifted back into twelve-year-old mode. "Would you *quit?*"

Diane chided herself silently. "I apologize. Actually, I admire your willingness to mend fences."

"The problem is, I didn't do anything wrong. She just got mad for no reason," Brittany complained.

Diane respected her daughter's opinion, but couldn't agree. "I'm sure she has her side to the story."

Josh gestured in frustration. "I don't pretend to know what happened, but she feels put-upon and insecure. It's partly a function of being an adolescent and partly my fault, I'm afraid."

That startled Diane. Josh hadn't intentionally caused their breach, and he was one of the best fathers she knew.

Brittany regarded him dubiously. "How can it be your fault?"

"When I was a kid, my family moved a lot, so we were always living among strangers," he explained. "Even when you're grown up, old emotions retain their power. I'm afraid I may have communicated my sense of being an outsider to my daughter. It's made her hypersensitive to anything that smacks of rejection."

He'd drawn that conclusion by himself? And had the courage to share it with her and Brittany? The last of Diane's resentment vanished.

So this was how couples patched up their differences—by examining their own motives and then being honest with those close to them.

"That's quite an insight," she said. "I'm impressed, Josh."

Her daughter clasped her hands tightly. "I'm sorry if she feels like we don't care about her. That's not true. Would you tell her that?"

"I'd be happy to. Now, if you don't mind, may I speak to your mother alone?" He waited politely for Brittany's permission.

"Okay. I've got stuff to do in my room." Brittany cast Diane a stern gaze. "Be *nice!*" With that, she took off.

Diane's sides hurt from trying not to laugh aloud. She'd hate for her daughter to overhear and mistake her amusement for mockery.

Josh grinned. "Your daughter's a sweetheart. But then, that's obvious, isn't it?"

"The problem is, sometimes she acts as if she's turning into *my* mother." Diane chuckled. "Do sit down. I promise to be on my best behavior. Otherwise, she might storm back and send me to my room."

After glancing at one of the photos of Will—there *were* a lot of them, weren't there?—Josh perched on the sofa's thick arm. "By the way, Dr. Kenton called me about Carly. There was another problem with misusing the camera. I informed my daughter she's going to be leaving it home for a while."

"Is she very upset?"

"She asked to change schools again, but she sounded miserable about the prospect. I told her I'm restricting the camera, regardless of where she's enrolled." He heaved a sigh. "We need to get her back on track. Reconciling with Brittany would be an excellent start, but she needs more."

"I'll do whatever I can." In response to his frankness, Diane added, "Josh, I realize I overreacted about the cottage. You're entitled to your opinion."

"Even if it is inane and uncalled for?" he joked.

She had to admire his sense of humor. "Okay, I admit, I'm totally prejudiced when it comes to this neighborhood. I love every inch of it. But Josh, I've been unfair to you and Carly."

He waved away the apology. "Let's put that behind us. I want us to be friends again."

"Me, too." Warmth suffused her as they sat together, simply enjoying the peace between them. Even though this moment might not last, Diane was grateful for the current reconciliation.

Josh broke the silence. "I have a proposition."

"Oh?" Diane felt suddenly wary. "What sort of proposition?"

Josh stretched his shoulders. "Let's go away for the weekend."

"What?" Had he misconstrued their situation? They were friends—good friends—but surely nothing more.

"Don't panic," he teased her. "I mean all four of us. A change of scenery often puts a new slant on things. Since the forecast calls for a heat wave, how about a trip to the beach?"

They could drive down to Newport or Huntington in forty-five minutes. "For a whole weekend? That's hardly necessary."

"You don't like the beach?"

"I love it." Suntan lotion, bare skin and relaxation.

He nodded. "Oliver's offered to loan us his cottage in Oceanside next weekend." The San Diego County community lay a little over an hour's drive south of Brea. "Three bedrooms and a kitchen."

A weekend for just the four of them. No neighbors poking into their business; no mom and sister across the street. No other friends to inspire Carly's jealousy.

Splendid for the girls. As for Diane and Josh, perhaps they could find a few moments alone. Just to talk, of course. Just to enjoy being friends. "That would be lovely. Thank you for arranging it."

"We can leave Friday evening if that suits you." Josh

eased to his feet. "And don't thank me. You're doing Carly and me a favor."

"This will be good for Brittany, too." They hadn't gone on a just-for-fun excursion in a long time. *Not since before Will died.*

"Let's consider this a fresh beginning," Josh said gently. "I'm sorry if I stepped on your toes. I'm not always the most socially smooth guy in the world."

"There's a lot to be said for diamonds in the rough." Diane hadn't meant to get so personal. "We could all use a weekend away."

"I'll go break the news to my daughter."

"Me, too."

He cast a parting gaze at Diane, which for an instant, smoldered with tenderness. Or perhaps she'd misread it.

As Josh departed through the slider, Diane's heart was beating faster than usual. She hoped he hadn't noticed. Her responses to this man were so unpredictable, she didn't even understand them herself.

Had she made a mistake by agreeing to spend a weekend with him? Even though he was gone, his masculine scent still filled the air. She'd have to be careful around him in Oceanside.

"Mom?"

Startled, she swung to face her daughter. "Did you hear? Mr. Armstrong is going to let us stay at his beach place next weekend."

"Wow!" Brittany's eyes flew wide. "You mean the one where Renée went?"

Diane nodded. "Mr. Lorenz and Carly are going with us."

"Awesome!" She hesitated then. "What if a baking order comes in?"

"You can't be on the job every weekend. You haven't actually promised anything, have you?"

"No."

Diane drew her into a hug. "You're so conscientious. I'm proud of you."

"That's just the way I am," Brittany said.

"So do you think you and Carly can get along?"

Her daughter wrinkled her nose. "She can be kind of a pain. I guess we'll work it out, though. I mean I love the beach. And I *am* sorry about upsetting her."

"That's my girl." Diane couldn't ask for more.

With an eager hop, her daughter headed for the stairs. "I'll take both my swimsuits. Don't forget to pack oversize towels. Should we bring two tubes of toothpaste or are we all sharing a bathroom?"

There was such a thing as being *too* responsible. "Brit!"

"What?"

"It's Monday. We aren't leaving yet. And if we forget anything, we can buy it there."

"I'll make sure we don't forget," returned her daughter, and disappeared from view.

This was going to be fun, Diane thought, and she felt even more grateful to Josh.

THE COTTAGE sat on the Strand, a narrow road running directly along the beach. This funky strip of small houses and apartments backed up to a cliff, above which lay the rest of the town, with its movie theaters, restaurants and military-themed shops serving the nearby Camp Pendleton Marine base.

As Josh's extended-cab pickup navigated the Strand on Friday evening, Diane rolled down her window to enjoy the sound of the ocean. The scent of brine wafted in, along with a cool breeze that dispelled the lingering inland heat.

En route, they'd sung old camp songs, including hokey rounds of "Row, Row, Row Your Boat" enlivened by Josh's baritone. Now, in the back, the girls giggled as they ogled a couple of Marines relaxing on a front porch. Despite some initial nattering about who sat where, the youngsters appeared to have resolved their differences.

Diane inhaled the aroma of fried chicken, which they'd bought after exiting the freeway. Their favorite junk food and a casual weekend—what a treat. She rested her head against the seat, glad to be alive.

And glad to be here with Josh and the girls. Perhaps for this weekend they could put any differences and awkward memories behind them.

"Can we go swimming right away?" Brittany asked.

"And freeze your tail off?" Diane replied. "It's getting cool out there."

"It's ninety!" her daughter replied.

"That was in Brea. It's cooler at the beach." By twenty or thirty degrees, she registered.

"The water's probably warm," Brittany pressed.

"The Pacific Ocean isn't a heated swimming pool," Josh deadpanned. "I have it on good authority that penguins suffer frostbite in these waters at night."

"There aren't any penguins," Brittany cried.

"Maybe it was pelicans."

Everyone laughed.

At the address Oliver had provided, they pulled off the Strand into a private space posted Authorized Cars Only. The cottage butted right against the sidewalk. You could stumble out the door after breakfast, trot across the narrow road and race over the sand to the surf.

Josh unlocked the car doors. As the girls piled out, he commanded, "Nobody goes anywhere until we've unloaded and eaten dinner. Everybody carry something."

"You don't have to tell me. As if I'd leave my stuff sitting out here unattended!" Brittany jumped down from the cab, with Carly behind her.

Diane joined the others in retrieving their suitcases and groceries from beneath a tarp on the truck bed. Josh hauled down a couple of foam body boards, plus volleyballs and flippers. Diane's contribution to the common good included sunscreen, towels and a bottle of ammonia-based window cleaner in case of jellyfish stings. Brittany had read about that on the Internet.

They'd neglected the shark repellent and scuba gear, Diane reflected wryly. But not much else.

"You'd think we were going to be here for weeks instead of a few nights," she commented as they mounted the porch.

"We could skip school and stay." Carly clearly relished that notion.

"Let's call in sick," Brittany agreed.

Josh unlocked the cottage, releasing a draft of slightly stale air laced with the scent of old popcorn. "That's what we forgot," Diane said. "Microwave popcorn."

He snapped his fingers. "No problem. Renée left a box in the pantry. She said we're free to use it."

"Then we're set."

Humming, Diane transferred milk and yogurt from a cooler into the fridge, while Josh helped the girls sort out bedrooms. Although Brittany could have shared Diane's room, she chose to stay with Carly.

This trip was already working wonders.

They ate supper around a slightly shaky kitchen table. Diane's legs kept brushing Josh's and, after initial efforts to avoid the contact, she gave in and rested her bare feet against his jeans. The girls, who were peering through a side window at a group of college-age people next door, didn't notice.

Afterward, as the last rays of sunset faded, the four of them strolled along the water's edge, wearing sweaters against the evening chill. Brittany paced ahead with Carly, who snapped photos of dog walkers and romantic couples. Against the panorama of sea and sky, the girls appeared as silhouettes.

"How can you take pictures when the light's fading?" Brit's voice drifted back above the waves.

"I've got a special setting. Wait'll you see how great it looks."

"You should put the camera down and just experience this. It's so pretty out here."

Beside Diane, Josh murmured, "That's a good idea. Think she'll listen?" He leaned close, blocking the breeze.

"We can always hope." If she turned, their lips might meet. *So I won't. We're just here to have fun.*

But that would *be fun,* declared a rebellious part of her brain.

"I *am* experiencing everything," Carly protested.

"Is it really so scary to put the lens aside? Try it."

Carly stuck the camera into her bag. "Okay. Satisfied?"

"Let's see how long you last. You're addicted."

"Am not!"

The girls pelted ahead, eager to get to nowhere in particular. The future, Diane supposed. Or perhaps just the pier, with its gleaming lights.

"She really might suffer withdrawal." Josh's hand closed around Diane's. She hadn't expected that, yet it felt right. Tantalizing.

Just for tonight, Diane took comfort in this man's company, in the escape from the loneliness that had enfolded her for too long. It had become second nature so much that she'd scarcely recognized it.

They strolled all the way to the pier, perhaps half a mile. Diane saw her daughter poke Carly, who glanced back. Quickly, she and Josh separated, but their handholding had been noticed.

The youngsters ducked their heads. She gathered they were giggling together.

At least they didn't appear to object.

The four of them climbed a steep outdoor staircase to the street at the top of the bluff. From there, they circled back to the cottage, where they settled on the porch with a bag of potato chips and watched moonlight sparkle on the waves. The girls squeezed around Josh on the glider, snuggling against him contentedly as he pointed to constellations. In the distance, she saw running lights twinkling as a boat headed toward the dark mountainous shape of Catalina Island, which was framed against the blue-black sky.

What a special evening. Even after the girls began to yawn and exhaustion claimed the adults, the magic stayed with Diane.

Chapter Thirteen

Josh stretched into wakefulness in the clear morning light. He'd kicked the covers off the bed and one ankle registered a trace of sand that had insinuated itself between the sheets.

Despite the minor discomforts, he'd rather be here than anywhere else in the world. Except for one place he could think of—which lay only a few dozen feet away.

If only he were waking up beside Diane. While most of the night's dreams had fled, he retained an impression of soft hair floating across his face and silken skin against his cheek. He'd been with her in spirit, if not in the flesh.

Despite his awareness of the emotional dangers, he sensed a growing excitement between the two of them. Not merely sexual, but profound in ways he'd never experienced with a woman—and that she might never have fully explored even with her husband. Otherwise, why did he detect those hints of innocence, of confusion, of almost unbearable hunger?

Restlessly, Josh threw on a robe, grabbed some clothes and, after checking the hallway, ducked into the bathroom. Crumpled towels told him that the girls had been here already.

He turned on the shower, hoping for a deliciously hot drenching, and instead was hit with a tepid spray. Blame an undersized water heater and the personal habits of females. Still, he got the job done.

When he emerged, shorts and T-shirt clinging to damp skin, he found the house empty. The creak of the glider drew him to the porch.

"Hi, Daddy!" Returned to the merry girl of years past, his daughter perched atop the railing with a bowl of cereal. She'd actually found a decent pair of jeans and a modest tank top to put on.

Brittany sat scribbling in a notebook. On the glider, Diane was grading papers.

"What's this? Working?" Josh pretended to chide. "It violates a local ordinance."

"Can't be helped, I'm afraid." Diane smiled up at him. "Look at the sleepyhead. I guess the salt air agrees with you."

He'd forgotten to put on his watch. "Is it late?"

"Dad, it's past nine!"

He claimed a box of cereal and dropped down beside Diane, then had to grab her papers to keep them from scattering. "This might be better handled indoors. And later. Say, next month."

"Dream on." Diane assembled them into a stack and clipped them together firmly. Despite her attention to duty, she seemed younger and more carefree than usual.

"We're making plans," Brittany informed Josh as he popped a handful of cereal into his mouth. "Legoland's just down the road in Carlsbad. We're a little old for that sort of thing, but we wouldn't have to tell anybody we went."

"I'm sorry?" To Josh, the statement made no sense.

"In other words, you'd like to go but you're embarrassed," Diane translated.

Thank goodness someone around here spoke adolescent.

"Right now, how about body surfing?" Josh asked. "As soon as I finish eating, that is."

"If we're sticking around here, I'd rather go shopping at the army surplus store." Carly had pointed one out when they arrived yesterday. "I've got enough money for a camouflage cap with a visor."

"So you can become a complete geek?" Brittany teased.

"I wonder if we could find camouflage aprons." In a burst of generosity, Carly added, "Let's buy an extra one for Suzy."

"Great idea. That could be sort of a uniform for Carly's Catering."

Delighted at the cooperation between the girls, Josh settled back and slipped his arm around Diane's shoulders. To his satisfaction, she laid her cheek on his shoulder.

In the pocket of Diane's skirt, the cell phone rang. "Who would call us *here?*" Brittany grumbled.

Exactly Josh's sentiment. Although a couple of his crews were on the job today, he'd designated a foreman to handle any problems and had left instructions that he was to be contacted only in case of emergency. *And it had better involve serious injury, a major fire or the possibility of a lawsuit,* he'd added.

Diane checked the screen. "It's my friend Nancy Yoshida, the one whose family used to own your house. Except she's Nancy Benedict now. I left a message that we were going to be down this way." She hurried indoors to talk, away from the rumble of the waves.

"She and her family live about half an hour south of here," Brittany explained. "I guess Mom's hoping you can meet them."

Losing his taste for cereal, Josh closed the lid. Share their getaway with others? Might as well have stayed home.

Carly scowled into her bowl. "I thought this weekend was just for the four of us."

Amazing how closely her mood mirrored Josh's. He'd never before realized how strongly his mood affected her. No wonder she'd picked up on his emotions after the spat at the community potluck.

"Yeah. Me, too," Brittany said. "I like Nancy's son and daughter. They're close to our age. But today, I just wanted to hang."

Carly tossed spare bits of cereal to a half-dozen birds poking around on the sidewalk. They pecked at the food and at each other until the smallest seized a trophy and escaped. "I wish your mom hadn't contacted them." She seemed reassured by Brittany's statement, though.

Diane emerged, still talking into the phone. "I'll ask the girls and call you back," she was saying. "That's really generous, Nancy."

Josh's spirits sank. He hoped she hadn't invited them to her house for dinner. Had Diane forgotten the steaks in the refrigerator? Surely she could visit her friend some other weekend.

"How'd you kids like to spend the afternoon at the San Diego Zoo?" Diane asked, tucking the phone into her pocket. "They have adorable baby animals and a couple of rare giant pandas on loan from China."

"We'd rather not." Brittany glanced at Carly, who nodded. "Besides, Mom, didn't you take your class to the Santa Ana Zoo last week? You'll be all zooed out."

"Oh, Josh and I aren't included. This is just for you kids to get acquainted," Diane said. "Nancy suggested we grownups could use a little time to ourselves." She halted, a trace of pink coloring her cheeks.

This friend proposed to whisk Carly and Brittany away, and

Diane hadn't objected? Suddenly, Josh couldn't believe his luck. "I'll bet you two could still find a chance to swing by the army surplus store afterward."

"What about swimming?" his daughter demanded.

"We can swim in the morning. We aren't leaving until tomorrow afternoon." Diane leaned against the doorframe. "Nancy and her family spent the night in Newport Beach with her brother, so they can collect you girls on their way home. We'll drive down to the zoo later and pick you up."

"I've never even met these people," Carly remarked irritably. "Let's just stay here."

Brittany glanced thoughtfully from her mother to Josh. "The zoo *is* world famous."

"I don't care— I'll pass."

Brittany beckoned Carly with a crooked finger. "I need to talk to you. Inside."

"Why?"

"Because it's *private*."

His daughter hesitated. Finally, she yielded. "Oh, all right." She stumped into the house behind her friend.

Josh closed the box of cereal. "Is there something going on between them that I haven't grasped?"

"I'm afraid Brittany's matchmaking," Diane said. "But I wouldn't mind getting away from the girls for a while."

"Neither would I." Not by a long shot.

A few moments later, the girls sauntered out. Brittany wore an expression of round-eyed innocence, while Carly appeared to be fighting a grin.

"Well?" Diane regarded them.

"Okay," Brit said.

"We'll go," Carly agreed.

"Great!"

The girls exchanged glances, then darted into the house, giggling. Diane shook her head in amusement. "Those two are hilarious."

"Why do I feel as if I'm caught in a remake of *The Parent Trap?*" Josh joked.

"Oh, I'm sure they don't take any of this seriously. But they do seem relieved that we're not at arm's length anymore."

"So am I."

"Me, too."

To Josh, those simple words spoke volumes. They were in this together, almost like two kids themselves, making their escape.

While Diane called to inform her friend that the girls had agreed to go, Josh went to put away the cereal. As he passed, she gave him a warm smile.

A pleasant shiver of anticipation accompanied him into the house.

STANDING on the porch, Diane waved goodbye to an SUV full of youngsters. Despite a twinge of guilt at such self-indulgence, she looked forward to spending the day with Josh.

Here at the beach, away from familiar settings and friends, all ordinary rules seemed suspended. They were free to have fun and let go of the usual concerns.

As the vehicle rounded the bend and disappeared, Josh's arm encircled her waist. For a moment, she relished the contact, then reluctantly withdrew.

"Sorry," he told her.

"Nothing to be sorry about." She knew that might be interpreted as encouragement. Right now, she almost wanted to encourage him.

A few stolen kisses. Perhaps more…

How could she explain her sense of excitement, as if she were an overgrown teenager instead of a woman of thirty-three? As if she'd never been touched before.

At this moment, her life with Will seemed far away and long ago. She really *didn't* have much experience with men.

She'd learned a great deal from Josh already, about communicating, about meeting each other halfway. How much more did she have the courage to learn?

"Are you all right?" he asked.

"Of course."

"Well, you weren't moving," he said lightly.

"I was thinking." She stared out at the ocean, dotted with surfers this morning.

"About what?"

She swallowed. "I don't know what I'm doing."

"Could you be more specific?"

"I don't know what I'm doing with you. What you expect. What *I* expect." Her hands clenched on the railing. "I suppose we could have a picnic. Or take in a movie."

"Or make love," he said, standing close behind her.

Diane could hardly breathe. "Is that... Did I give the impression...?"

"Or we could play cards," Josh continued in the same calm tone.

Diane turned and met the teasing challenge in his eyes. "You think I'm afraid."

"To play cards?"

"No!" To make love. Then the truth hit home. She *was* afraid. "I realize I'm a mother and all that, but in some ways I'm not very experienced."

"There's a cure for that," he murmured, his voice tingling across her nerve endings.

"Josh, I fell in love with Will in high school. I've only had a relationship with one guy."

Gently, he led her to the glider. "In case you're wondering, I haven't made any assumptions about what we're going to do."

She sat beside him, trying to sort out her feelings as she relaxed against his shoulder. Did she dare yield to her longings and be intimate with this man, knowing how complicated everything would be?

Life didn't come with guarantees. Except one, she reflected. That if she retreated out of cowardice, this chance might never come again.

"Maybe you should," she told him. "Make assumptions, I mean."

He shifted her onto his lap. "How's that for starters?"

His hardness and heat radiated through her. "People will see!" Embarrassed, she glanced toward the sidewalk and a couple of dog walkers who had just gone by.

"Do you know those people? Will you ever see them again?"

"No." Besides, at the beach people often snuggled in public, and no one seemed to notice. "I must strike you as awfully timid. It's just inexperience, I guess."

"The word I'd choose would be *innocent*. I like that," Josh said. "It makes me want to protect you."

As his arms closed around her, Diane had the sense of teetering on a threshold. Beyond lay the danger of a broken heart and masses of regret. With Will, she'd never doubted they would spend their whole lives together. With Josh, she wasn't sure they'd still be close a month from now.

But she longed for him with a razor edge of desire and a rush of tenderness. She had to do this, if only for herself.

"No promises," she warned.

"I can handle that." Drawing her nearer, Josh ran his thumbs lightly up her rib cage, close to her breasts.

As hunger filled her, Diane touched his face and then, emboldened, kissed the pulse of his neck. As if he belonged to her. As if she had the right to touch him whenever she pleased.

And for today, she did.

"You were right," Josh murmured. "Let's take this indoors."

Diane felt a sudden burst of boldness. Sliding to her feet, she tugged on his hand. Once through the door, Josh whirled her across the living room. Diane lost her flip-flops en route. Barefoot and wild—totally unlike her usual self.

About to get a lot wilder.

In his bedroom, Josh caged her against the wall, his body moving over hers as his hands cupped her face. He tasted her mouth, igniting flares across Diane's body.

She kissed him back, savoring his strength and gentleness. Aching for more.

"Whose clothing shall we take off first?" he asked when they came up for air.

"You're the expert." She didn't quite finish the sentence, because he was kissing her again, his tongue arousing hers, his hips swaying as if they were responding to a Latin beat.

How wonderful and strange and enticing to caress this man. And what an incredible yearning he aroused.

With Will, they'd taken lovemaking slowly, building to the point where she was ready. With Josh, she'd been ready almost before they'd begun.

His palms stroked her breasts, hardening the nipples. With sudden resolve, she traced her hand down to his erection, and thrilled at his responding groan.

She'd never realized her entire body could quiver with

sexual hunger. That she could want a man with her hands and her thighs and…everything.

They tumbled onto the bed. "What was that nonsense about lacking experience?" Josh panted.

"You were right. There's a cure for that." Feverishly, she unzipped his pants while leaning forward so that he could unbutton her blouse.

"Oh, man. You're completely amazing." He eased back the blouse and unhooked her lacy bra. "Pink. I knew it!"

"Had me pegged, huh?"

"In my dreams."

He'd dreamed about her? The thought was thrilling. Then his lips captured a nipple, and Diane couldn't speak, couldn't think, only urge him on.

Yet he delayed, studying her through half-closed eyes. "Hurry," she whispered.

"Why? You're splendid. I want to enjoy you."

She grasped his hips. "I want to enjoy you, too."

"Getting there is half the fun."

"I want all the fun!"

Instead of complying, he stopped. "Damn. And I'm supposed to be experienced."

"What's wrong?"

To her dismay, he swung off the bed and rummaged through a drawer. "Where did I put them?

Condoms. How could she have forgotten?

Wait a minute… He'd deliberately brought them. Had he been expecting this or did he carry them everywhere?

Diane didn't care. At least he was behaving responsibly.

He produced a small packet. "Want me to help?" she offered.

"Better not. I'm so sensitive I might explode." He opened the package.

Properly protected, he returned to the bed. They kissed with growing fervor, his hands sliding over her curves. Eagerly, Diane arched, elation spiking as they joined.

They moved together, clinging and nuzzling, as his thrusts gradually gathered speed. The only lovemaking she'd known before had been gentle, a kind of spreading glow. But as Josh began to move hard and fast, he raised her to a realm of extraordinary sensation.

Diane melted into him, reveled in the expanding heat of her own body and the spicy perfume of their lovemaking. She lost all awareness of anything other than this bliss, a great explosion of it that seemed to carry her forward forever.

At last she sank into a state of utter peace, almost floating beside Josh. She scarcely recognized this sexual woman. How had she kept such passion bottled inside for so long?

They murmured to each other, sharing little observations with the intimacy she'd missed so keenly, until a powerful drive swelled again. The second time lasted longer, lifting Diane to even greater heights.

Afterward, she lay against Josh, treasuring his scent and the newly familiar shape of his thighs and chest. To her great relief, she didn't feel disloyal to Will for a response that transcended anything they'd shared. Tragedy and maturity had shaped her into a different person. It seemed only natural that she responded differently to this man and this relationship.

Because they *did* have a relationship. The understanding that it might not last only added to the poignancy.

For the next few hours, Diane refused to think about anything except Josh and how good it felt to soap each other in the shower and walk hand-in-hand on the beach. After they climbed the steps to the top of the cliff, they snacked on tacos that tasted better than a hundred-dollar dinner. Or what Diane imagined a hundred-dollar dinner would taste like, if she ever consumed one.

Back at the cottage, they sprawled on the sofa, legs entwined, reading side by side, sharing passages from their books. When Josh read a funny section aloud, Diane found his deep rumble so magnetic that she almost missed the point of the anecdote.

Later, as planned, they drove to San Diego, where they found Brittany brimming with good humor and Carly eager to display animal photos in her viewfinder. Nancy seemed fascinated to meet Josh, but tactfully she confined her conversation to events at the zoo.

Back in Oceanside the four of them stopped by the army surplus store, where the girls made their purchases. After a quick dinner, they went to the movies and passed a giant tub of popcorn back and forth like any family.

Diane couldn't remember a more perfect day.

On Sunday morning, Josh led the little band in an early-morning shell-hunting expedition on the beach. When the morning fog lifted, they swam, tumbling playfully in the light waves. The water was mild, and except for a handful of surfers in the distance, they had the shore to themselves.

If only they could stay longer. But there was packing to do, and the cottage must be restored to pristine condition.

Functioning as a team, the foursome washed a load of sheets and towels, vacuumed the carpet and scrubbed the kitchen and bathrooms. "It's worth it," Brittany said. "Let's be really nice to Oliver so he'll let us come again."

Carly agreed wholeheartedly.

After lunch, Diane settled into the truck's front seat, wincing at the sore muscles produced by the weekend's activities. That had been well worth it, too.

When her cell phone rang, she checked the display. "It's my mom." Puzzled, she answered the call as the truck moved forward. "What's up?"

"I thought I'd better warn you." Lois sounded grim. "Your sister's upset, and I'm afraid you and Josh are in for a bit of a shock."

"Why?" Diane kept her face as blank as possible to hide her sudden rush of concern. *Please don't let anything spoil our wonderful time together.*

"It was in the paper this morning. The man who killed Will got shot to death last night during a robbery," her mother said. "The clerk got hurt, too. There was another gang member involved. I'm sorry to say we were right to think the worst of Hector Fry."

"I see." But Diane didn't, not really. Her mother filled her in as painful fragments of memory swarmed: the horrifying moment when Will had collapsed onto the sidewalk, the ambulance racing to the hospital, the anguish when she learned he was really gone, and then the whole miserable trial.

How on earth was she going to break this news to her companions?

Chapter Fourteen

Despite the challenge of navigating his truck onto the freeway, Josh didn't miss the dismay in Diane's voice. "Is your mom okay?" he asked as soon as she closed the phone.

"She's fine." She stared dully through the windshield.

Well, *something* was obviously wrong.

"Mom?" Brittany leaned forward from the rear seat. "What did Grandma tell you?"

Diane blinked and inhaled deeply, as if emerging from a trance. A glance at Josh was all the warning he received before she plunged ahead.

"Hector Fry, the man who killed Dad, got shot to death last night."

An image of the young man sprang into Josh's memory, at the defense table and on the witness stand. Polite and clean-shaven, he'd seemed younger than his nineteen years and sincere about renouncing gang violence. Josh had found his story of the gun going off by accident quite plausible.

"He and another gang member robbed a convenience store and injured the young man working at the counter. The police confronted him and shots were fired."

"He *was* still in a gang when he killed Dad. He deliberately shot into a crowd." Brittany cried. "That liar!"

"I don't understand," Carly said. "What's this all about?"

Diane shook her head at the girls. "We can go into it later."

Josh felt as if someone had punched him in the gut. For two years, he'd believed that he'd done the right thing by giving an innocent kid a second chance. Unless other facts came to light about this recent tragedy, it seemed he'd been tragically mistaken.

Hector and his lawyer had presented a convincing story about the youth's determination to go straight and his devotion to his cancer-stricken mother, Delores. At least, they'd convinced Josh. Normally, he prided himself on being logical and realistic. How could he have made such a huge error in judgment?

A short while ago, he'd enjoyed the prospect of driving home with the four of them in close proximity. Now, he wished he and Diane were alone so he could apologize from the bottom of his heart.

Instead all he said was, "How's the clerk doing? Is he going to recover?"

"He was in surgery, the last Mom heard." Diane spoke with a flatness that revealed her stunned state.

"Somebody killed your dad?" Carly asked Brittany.

Josh's stomach knotted. The whole ugly business was about to come out. He hadn't considered how learning about his role might affect their daughters.

"He was walking with my mom at a street fair in Fullerton." Brittany's voice shook. Although Josh recalled from the trial that she'd been staying with her grandmother that night, the loss clearly remained vivid. "This creep, Hector, was aiming at rival gang members and he killed my father."

"They never caught him?"

"Oh, they caught him!" Brittany squirmed in her seat.

"But he told a bunch of lies in court and one of the jurors believed him."

"They let him go?" Disbelief colored Carly's question.

Brittany's shoulders hunched. "Yeah. I'm glad he's dead."

"Me, too."

Abruptly, Josh recalled the defense attorney asking during jury selection whether anyone had watched a close relative die of cancer. Several of the jurors, including Josh, had answered yes. During the summation, the lawyer had repeatedly made eye contact with each of them.

On the stand, Hector had spoken earnestly of his mother's terminal illness and her profound vulnerability. He'd claimed she'd bought the gun because she feared someone might break in while she was home alone. During the street fair, he'd said, relatives left their five-year-old at the apartment and the child got hold of it.

When Hector tried to snatch it away, it had fired out the window. The five-year-old was too young to be a coherent witness, and Hector's mother had died before the trial began.

Why did I believe him?

Because, Josh realized, listening to Hector describe his mother's suffering had triggered a vivid recollection of his own brother wasting away, and of his sense of helplessness. Just as the attorney intended, he'd empathized with Hector.

They played me. And I bought right into their lies.

As a result, Hector lay dead and a sales clerk was in the hospital. And Josh had hurt the people he loved most in the world.

He switched on the radio. "Okay if we listen for news? I'd like to find out how the clerk's doing."

"Of course," Diane said.

In the rearview mirror, Josh glanced at Brittany. The tears that glimmered in her eyes felt like a reproach.

This weekend, the four of them had developed a wonderful closeness. He only hoped it wasn't lost forever.

AFTER A SERIES of commercials and other news, the radio announcer updated the clerk's condition. To Diane's relief, he'd survived surgery and was in stable condition.

"What does stable mean?" Brittany asked.

"He's not in immediate danger," Diane said. "If he were, they'd describe him as critical."

She didn't dare look at Josh. He'd barely spoken since he'd heard about the incident, except to inquire after the young man.

She wasn't sure what she'd have said to him, anyway. The news had jolted her back to the wrenching hours after Will's shooting. Just when she'd believed those events lay safely in the past, they'd come crashing into the present.

Yet, to her surprise, she felt no anger toward Josh. When her mother had suggested that she forgive him, Diane hadn't seen how she could.

That was before she'd learned that couples had to accept each other's flaws, and acknowledge their own, in order to resolve their differences. And that you didn't have to be in synch on every topic to have a rich and supportive relationship. Along the way, she'd come to understand that, even though he'd been wrong, Josh had entertained a reasonable doubt. He'd followed his conscience, as a juror ought to do.

But how was she going to explain all this to Brittany? In her desire to avoid arousing conflict, Diane, too, had made a mistake. She should have leveled with Brittany about Josh right away.

Once they got home, Diane decided, she was going to have to take her daughter aside and explain the situation in as gentle a manner as possible. Frank discussions among the four of them might even deepen the bond that had been formed this weekend.

The girls settled down during the drive, and seemed only slightly subdued by the time Josh halted in front of Diane's house. "I hate for the weekend to be over, but I suspect the girls have homework."

Carly groaned. "Don't remind me."

Brittany grabbed her suitcase. "I can't wait to see all the photos from this weekend. Will you e-mail me the best ones?"

"Absolutely!"

From the truck bed, Josh removed Diane's suitcase, cooler and beach gear. "I'll carry these inside."

"Thanks." Quietly, she added, "We should talk."

After a glance to make sure the girls were out of earshot, he murmured, "I'm sorry about all this. More than I can say."

"Me, too." She was about to suggest they arrange to meet later that night when she caught sight of her sister slamming out of the house across the street.

The instant she saw Sarah's face, Diane knew they were in for trouble.

THE CRASH of the front door at number 2 was all the warning Josh received before a shorter version of Diane, chestnut hair flying and fire snapping in her eyes, pounded toward them.

He'd felt the blaze of Sarah Oldham's anger throughout the trial. She'd glared at every defense witness, including an aging aunt who'd praised Hector's devotion to his mom. In the corridor, after the judge had dismissed the jury, she'd accosted Josh in near hysteria, demanding an explanation. He'd been grateful when the bailiff cautioned her to respect the integrity of the jury system.

At the community potluck, she'd greeted him politely but

distantly. Given the lingering coolness, he'd suspected that he would have to deal with her eventually. But did it have to be under such painful circumstances, and in front of the girls, who'd paused on the porch in confusion?

Diane raised one hand to stop her sister. "This isn't the time or place."

"This is exactly the time and place!" Sarah confronted Josh. "Now will you admit you were wrong? How many innocent people have to get shot before the truth penetrates your thick head?"

The girls regarded her in dismay. "What's she talking about, Mom?" Brittany asked.

Sarah blinked. Perhaps she hadn't considered the impact of her accusation on the youngsters. "You didn't tell her?"

"I was planning to handle that with maturity and tact, qualities that are obviously in short supply around here," Diane snapped.

"You should have done it *before* you made the mistake of welcoming this man into your life!" Sarah flared.

"How I arrange my personal life is my business."

Josh appreciated Diane's standing by him. If only he could issue a heartfelt apology and banish the whole issue, he would. But Sarah appeared in no mood to be pacified and, besides, her public tirade had already complicated matters.

"Mom?" Brittany repeated.

"I'll explain inside." Diane steered her daughter toward the door. When Sarah started to follow, she received a sharp rebuff. "You are not welcome in my house until you apologize for your behavior."

"My behavior? What about him?" Sarah demanded childishly.

Josh could scarcely bear the bewilderment on Brittany's

and Carly's faces. He decided to defuse the situation, at least temporarily, by leaving. "We're going home." He'd explain this to his daughter in his own way.

Diane gave him a subtle nod of agreement. At least she wasn't shutting him out.

He and a puzzled Carly climbed into the truck. Sarah swung about and marched away. Going to e-mail all her friends and spread the gossip, Josh supposed.

The ripple effect might be only beginning.

IF DIANE hadn't been so preoccupied with Brittany, she'd have run after her sister and told her…what? To mind her own business? She'd already done that.

She understood Sarah's reaction. Five years ago, when their father had suffered his fatal stroke, Will had stood by them in the hospital, a rock on whom the rest of them had depended. Afterward, he'd assisted Lois with the funeral, and had prayed with them every evening for weeks. Still the baby of the family at twenty-four, Sarah had been especially comforted by his presence.

His murder had hit Sarah as if she were losing her father all over again. But how unfair to unload on Josh.

In the living room, Brittany dropped her suitcase and began pacing. "Carly's dad was on the jury? He was the holdout?"

"Yes," Diane confirmed. "I had a hard time accepting it, too, but I've come to understand he was obeying his conscience."

"You shouldn't be friends with him!" Tears coursed down the girl's cheeks. "I trusted him—and you."

Diane's heart squeezed. "I was wrong not to tell you, honey. But Josh *is* trustworthy. What a mess for everybody. Carly's bound to be upset, too."

"She didn't know?"

"She wasn't even aware that your father had been murdered, remember?"

Her hands clenched into fists. "Well, he should have told her the whole story. And you should have told me, too."

"I agree. I'm sorry." Diane struggled to offer some perspective. "Sweetheart, grownups don't have a lock on the best way to deal with everything. We do what we believe is best, but we all make mistakes."

"Does Josh know he messed up?"

"Yes. He apologized to me in the truck. He must feel terrible about having been so deceived."

"All the same..." Brittany blinked away her tears. "I don't want to hate him. I really don't."

"Josh didn't mean hurt us," Diane assured her.

Her daughter stopped pacing. "The pastor says to forgive people who wrong us."

Her maturity was impressive. "He's right, although I know that's asking a lot."

"I'll try. And I promise not to hold this against Carly." Brittany lifted her chin stubbornly. "But Mom, we can never let him take Dad's place. He doesn't belong in our family. That would be disloyal."

Oh, dear. That was the heart of the problem, wasn't it? "This isn't a question of loyalty. It's not as if he hurt Will. He just..."

"Mom, you can't side with him!"

"I won't. I'd never put anyone ahead of you." She had to stand by Brittany through this crisis. And it *was* a crisis, threatening not only Diane's connection with Josh but her daughter's trust.

Brittany came first. Josh of all people should understand that.

MONDAY'S NEWSPAPER brought the welcome news that the clerk's condition continued to improve. It also cited the less palatable information that, according to police reports, Hector had resumed his gang activity almost immediately following his acquittal. And that, most likely, he had never really dropped his affiliation.

As if Josh required any reason to feel worse, Diane called to explain that, for Brittany's sake, they'd have to cool things for a while. She'd been regretful, and so was he.

He didn't plan to give up. But he had his own problems.

Carly had received his account with shocked disbelief. "How will I ever face Brittany again?"

"I've talked to her mother. She's being remarkably understanding about this."

"Yes, but Dad, I can imagine what I'd think if somebody else's father had done this!" his daughter protested.

"Try to put yourself in my shoes." He needed to explain this clearly. "Jurors don't get special training or require any qualifications. They're just ordinary citizens trying to do their best. To make things even harder, they have to base their decision solely on what's presented in evidence. No independent research, no opportunity to demand the full story."

"The other eleven people figured it out."

She was right about that. "Yes, they did. If I had a time machine, I'd go back and change my vote."

"Fat lot of good that does."

He hadn't scolded her for her anger. Well-intentioned or not, his actions had created a disruption that had touched a lot of people, and now they were creating problems for Carly. He hoped that her fundamental faith in him hadn't been shaken.

Could she and Brittany ever restore their friendship? And she desperately needed Diane's influence as a role model.

He needed Diane, too. To laugh with, to talk to and hold. She hadn't merely breached his defenses, she'd freed him from a self-imposed prison. With her, he'd experienced a new kind of emotional freedom. He'd begun to feel that he might finally fit into a family again.

He and Carly simply had to ride out the storm. Sadly, it showed no signs of clearing by Monday afternoon when he picked her up after school.

She slumped in her seat. "I'm not going back to Brea Academy. You can't make me."

Was this his fault, or a continuation of her previous problems? "Brittany told them about my role on the jury?"

"Somebody read the name of the juror on the Internet. Those kids have been together since kindergarten—they're practically a family," she burst out as the truck inched through traffic. "They all hate me."

He wished he could spare his daughter this fallout. "How did Brittany act?"

"She sat with me at lunch." That had been kind. "But she didn't ask about the beach photos or mention getting together. I can tell she's uncomfortable."

"She'll come to terms with it."

Carly plucked at her seat belt. "Mrs. Bittner went out of her way to be nice, too, but everybody figured she felt sorry for me."

Josh struggled to find the right words of comfort. "Too bad," was the best he managed.

"And I got a D on an English test. I couldn't concentrate. Don't tell me to do extra credit. I hate that whole snotty place!"

Transferring to a new school at this point would put her at a serious disadvantage, academically and socially. Josh almost wished he hadn't moved from La Habra in the first place. Still, she'd had a few issues there, too—particularly since she'd dyed her hair and started wearing those horrible clothes.

He wished he could have built his dreamhouse sooner.

Once they settled down for the long term… Well, how could he really be sure she'd fit into that school system, either? Raising kids wasn't easy, no matter where you lived.

And if he hadn't come to Brea, he might not have gotten to know Diane. In spite of everything, he didn't regret a minute of their friendship.

"Please stick it out for the rest of the semester," he urged. "If you still feel the same then, I'll see what I can arrange."

Carly lapsed into silence. Josh decided to phone Diane later and ask her advice.

They were going to weather this. They had to.

Driving into Harmony Circle usually soothed his spirits. Josh liked the orderly lawns and decorative plantings, and most of all the fact that Diane lived here. Although tempted to cruise past her house, however, he decided not to risk another confrontation with Sarah, and headed directly to number 18.

On the sidewalk a few doors down, Oliver and his cousin, Rafe Montoya, stood arguing. What was this about?

As Josh exited the truck, Rafe strode up and thrust a petition at him. "Sherry and Winston accepted Minnie's counteroffer. They're buying the cottage. This petition asks the city council to declare it a historic structure so they can't tear it down."

"I'll sign!" Carly hopped down on the passenger side.

"Sorry. Registered voters only." Rafe's dark gaze raked Josh, who studied the petition.

A scan of the names and addresses revealed most of the street's residents. Probably the only absentees were those who simply weren't home from work yet.

Oliver reached him. "This is wrong. For one thing, Brea's historic registry is supposed to be voluntary, not imposed by the neighbors."

"All you care about is that the sale goes through so you earn your commission," snapped his cousin.

"I'm not the only person who'd get hurt. It's unfair to Minnie's family."

"Somebody else will buy it."

"With so many restrictions, the value is bound to drop," Oliver pointed out.

Rafe folded his arms. His cousin's arguments obviously hadn't changed his mind.

Regretfully, Josh held out the petition. "I sympathize, but I can't sign this. It's unfair to Minnie *and* to the buyers to change the rules at this point."

"Fine." Rafe snatched the document from his hands. "Someone's messing with my block, and I don't intend to stand for it. Neither do most of the other residents." Scowling, he marched away.

Great. Josh had freed the man who killed Diane's husband, and now he was siding with people who wanted to destroy a beloved landmark. *Guess I wasn't destined to be Mr. Popularity.*

"Thanks," Oliver told him.

"You're welcome, but I didn't do it for your sake." Josh sighed. "I'm sticking by my principles. Although these days I'm not entirely sure that's such a good idea."

"It's always a good idea." If Oliver had heard about the jury business, he didn't seem fazed by it. "See you around."

"Guess so."

Indoors, Carly dropped her book bag with a thud. "Did it ever occur to you that you might be wrong about the cottage, like you were with Hector Fry?"

A low blow. "I'm staying the course," Josh said wearily.

"Just like you're forcing me to stay at the academy?" she demanded. "Did you know Brittany's dad was a teacher there?

Everyone talks about how wonderful he was. A couple of the kids started crying. I felt awful!"

"None of this is your fault."

"That's right. It's *your* fault." She thudded up the stairs. "That's why I'm calling Mom."

"Excuse me?" He couldn't imagine what any of this had to do with Tiffany.

"I'm going to stay with her and Al. They'll *have* to put me in another school."

"Honey, please don't…"

The door to her room slammed.

Josh's heart ached for her. Since the divorce, Carly had repeatedly spun fantasies about her mother transforming herself into the ideal mom. Even though Tiffany let her down again and again, his daughter clung to the delusion.

Worse, what if his ex-wife agreed? Their daughter might spend a few weeks there, long enough to interfere with her schooling, and then Josh had no doubt she'd come storming home amid even more turmoil.

What a mess.

In all honesty, he had to admit their position on Harmony Road wasn't likely to improve any time soon, not with this cottage controversy, and Carly seemed adamant about changing schools. Perhaps instead of putting his dream project on a back burner, he should hurry matters along.

If he brought in crews and scaled back the planned upgrades, Josh could get this house ready to sell in a few more months. Meanwhile, he could search for the right piece of land. With luck, it might already have a small house where they could live while he built the new one, or else they'd make do with a portable home for a while.

That meant moving farther away from Diane. His gut

twisted. But if their relationship was so fragile it could only survive while they lived next door, it probably wouldn't weather the current series of problems, anyway.

Much as the prospect distressed him, maybe it was time he quit fighting the inevitable and took Carly away.

Chapter Fifteen

In his home office, Josh clicked through real estate offerings on the Internet, searching for a piece of land large enough to suit his purposes. He didn't find anything remotely within his price range, even if he resigned himself to driving several hours a day to work.

Well, he hadn't expected to find it right off the bat. He'd ask Oliver to look for him.

Through the wall, he heard the murmur of Carly's voice as she responded to her mother on the phone. She seemed to be having difficulty getting a word in edgewise. What on earth was Tiffany yammering about? Couldn't she pick up on their daughter's strained emotions?

His ex-wife didn't always behave insensitively. There were moments when she rose above her frivolous upbringing, and he believed that, at some level, she truly cared about Carly. Not enough to seek custody, and he'd fight her in court if she tried. But at least she ought to be willing to lend a sympathetic ear.

Carly's footsteps in the hall alerted him to the fact that the conversation must have ended. He expected her to come tell him the results, but instead the stairs creaked beneath her, and then the front door opened and closed.

Where had she gone? Surely Tiffany hadn't arranged to pick her up. Josh couldn't ignore the possibility, though.

Grabbing his phone, he dialed his ex-wife's cell. Tiffany answered on the second ring.

"It's Josh. Carly just marched out of the house. What's going on?"

"I have no idea." From the background, he heard voices and tinny music. Not quite a party ambience—more like a mall. Tiffany's native habitat.

"You aren't coming to get her?"

"Why would I do that?"

Because your daughter begged you. But to be fair, he hadn't actually heard what Carly said. "I thought she called you to ask about visiting."

"She did mention staying with me for a while. I'm afraid it's impossible. Guess what I'm doing?" Tiffany's voice bubbled with excitement. "Shopping for maternity clothes. Al and I are having a baby!"

Oh, great. Carly desperately needed her mother's support, and instead she'd learned she was being replaced with a newer, cuter model. That might be putting the case harshly, but Josh suspected that's how the discovery felt to his daughter.

"Congratulations." He couldn't resist adding, "I thought Al didn't want more children." The investment banker had a couple of daughters by a previous marriage.

"He said he's got enough *girls*. We had in vitro, to make sure it's a son. Isn't that cool?"

Designer children to suit their ritzy lifestyle. Well, their values didn't concern Josh except for the effect on his daughter. "How did Carly take it?"

"She never says much."

Maybe she would if you tried listening. He refrained from

criticizing, however. "Inviting her to visit next weekend might reassure her that the baby isn't going to claim *all* your attention."

"I'm afraid we're much too busy. Ooh, you should see this adorable stroller! But I'm going to wait and buy one in New York."

"New York?" There seemed to be gaps in this conversation.

"Al's been promoted and transferred to bank headquarters. We're moving next month," Tiffany announced. "I've got so much to do, I can hardly keep track of it all. My gosh, I'd better get over to Saks and find a winter coat. It'll have to be big enough to cover the bulge. Did I mention I'm due in March?"

The picture became excruciatingly clear. Their distraught child had called in search of reassurance, and instead she'd been handed the news that her mother was abandoning her, physically and emotionally.

Scolding Tiffany would be as pointless as arguing with a cat. "Good luck in your new life."

"I'm sure we'll visit the West Coast occasionally. I promised Carly she'll meet her new brother before he's old enough to walk."

Impatience overwhelmed Josh's good intentions. "I'm sure that thrilled the hell out of her. Now if you'll excuse me, I'd better go pick up whatever pieces are left of our daughter's self-esteem."

He hung up and went downstairs, half expecting the phone to ring as his ex-wife called back to inquire what he'd meant. But she didn't.

Outside, darkness was falling. No sign of Carly.

Josh debated cruising the area. The girl was twelve, and they lived in a safe neighborhood. Surely she deserved some slack. Also, she'd come home when she got hungry.

Remembering the dirty clothes from the trip, Josh dug Carly's out of her bag and carted the lot downstairs. When his stomach began to rumble, he retrieved hot dogs and buns from the freezer along with a bag of green beans. That would cover their basic needs.

The phone rang. He answered with a brisk, "Josh here."

"It's Diane." A ripple of relief ran through him. *At least she's still speaking to me.* "I thought Brittany was okay, but she can't stop crying. Could we come over? It might help if she talks to you."

"Sure." He'd do his best. "But I'm surprised she'd want to."

"That's the problem—conflicting emotions. She's really grown attached to you, but her first love is for Will. She feels torn in half. That's my take, anyway."

And probably the right one. "I'm happy to do whatever I can."

"We'll be there in a minute."

Josh set aside the food. He didn't plan to eat until Carly was back home, in any case.

The pair arrived via the rear slope. Josh's throat tightened at the sight of Brittany's tear-streaked face. "Babe, I'm sorry."

She ducked inside with her head lowered. If she acknowledged his apology, he didn't hear her.

Diane still smelled of sea wind and sunshine. "We talked things over and she went up to unpack. She seemed to be fine, and then I heard her sobbing."

"What set you off?" Josh asked the girl, who huddled in an easy chair.

She wrapped her arms around herself. "I was looking at pictures from the birthday party, all of us laughing. I was so glad you were there."

"Me, too," he said.

"Well, I shouldn't have been. Because of Dad."

"I have the greatest respect for your father," Josh told her gently. "He must have been a wonderful man."

"I can't understand why you didn't go along with the rest of the jury. How could you feel sorry for that criminal, after what he did?"

Josh sat on the couch beside Diane, taking strength from her nearness. No use repeating the same old stuff about obeying his conscience. Although that was true it didn't satisfy anyone, including him. "I've been trying to figure out the same thing."

"What do you mean?" Diane laid her hand on his forearm, apparently without thinking, and then removed it.

"I consider myself a rational person," he began. "I thought I'd reached a logical, compassionate conclusion."

"It wasn't compassionate to my dad!" Brittany insisted.

"Let's hear him out, honey." Diane clasped her hands in her lap.

"In retrospect, I can see that I wasn't all that rational. I failed to take into account the fact that, contrary to what you may believe, I'm human," Josh told them wryly. "As your Mom's aware, Brittany, I grew up with a terminally ill brother. When you're focused on trying to protect someone so fragile, all your priorities get rearranged."

She frowned. "I don't understand."

"I used to run interference for Tim. Fight bullies at school. Give him the best part of my lunch because his appetite was so poor. Lie to kids about his illness, so they wouldn't write him off."

Brittany's eyes widened in sympathy. "What happened to him?"

"He died a long time ago," Josh answered. "When I sat through that trial, the possibility that my experience with Tim might affect my judgment never occurred to me."

Diane watched him intently. "You think it did?"

"Today, I kept trying to figure out how the defense persuaded me, what strategy they used." *And why I fell for it.*

"Hector Fry and his aunt emphasized his devotion to his mother, and how weak she'd become. It made sense to me that her son supported her desire to keep a gun in the house."

No one had ever proved where the weapon came from or who really owned it. The prosecutor had claimed the gun indicated Hector's continuing gang involvement.

"You gave him the benefit of the doubt because you thought he'd been protecting his mom," Brittany interpreted.

"Exactly. My experiences colored my reaction. I assumed the other jurors had simply never been desperate to ease the suffering of someone they loved."

"We were suffering, too."

"Of course you were. But I didn't have the power to bring your father back. Sending a man to prison for an accident— what I thought was an accident—would have been a terrible injustice." Josh had believed that passionately. "I had to choose, and I chose wrong."

Diane gave him a sad hint of a smile. "Misplaced empathy."

"Empathy and stupidity," he corrected. "Sarah's right. I'm an idiot. I apologize for all the hurt I put you through."

"Aunt Sarah's wrong," Brittany corrected. "You don't have a thick head. You have a soft heart."

Josh hadn't expected such kindness from a twelve-year-old. "Thank you. I hope we can be friends again."

"If I ever got sick, I'd want you taking care of me like you did your brother." Brittany wiped moisture from her cheek. "Is Carly around?"

They'd laid the topic to rest, at least temporarily. Thank goodness.

"She went for a walk. I expect her back any minute." Normally, Josh didn't share painful personal matters, but these two deserved the whole story, so he added, "Her mother and stepfather are expecting a baby and moving to New York. We just learned about that. I think Carly's hurt."

"She's probably out taking pictures. That'll make her feel better." Brittany sniffled, then waved away a tissue Diane offered. "Mom, I'm *okay*. I'm not going to start blubbering again."

"Okay." Her mother stuffed it into her pocket. "How long has Carly been gone?"

Guiltily, Josh realized he'd lost track of the time. "I'm not sure. At least an hour."

"Have you tried calling her?"

Good idea. "I'll do that."

He pressed the rapid-dial button on his phone, and from upstairs came the familiar rock tune that served as Carly's ring.

She'd left her cell behind. That was when Josh started to worry.

IF DIANE had to choose a moment when she discovered how much she loved Josh Lorenz, it was during that conversation with Brittany, when she watched him turn his heart inside out. How many people would be that honest, under any circumstances? And especially to a child?

If she had to choose a moment when she realized she might lose him, it occurred a short while later.

She'd accompanied him upstairs to see if Carly had taken her camera. It was still there. Stepping into the hall again, anxious about the girl, Diane almost didn't react to the sight of Josh's computer in the next room, its screen covered with real estate listings.

Why was he looking at properties? "What's that for?"

"Trying to find my dream lot."

"What's the point? It probably won't still be available when…" She noted the tightness in his expression. "I thought that wouldn't happen for a year or so."

He tilted his head apologetically. "Carly's desperately unhappy trying to fit into a school full of kids your husband taught, and she's stuck with a dad who rubs people the wrong way. We're both fish out of water." He mentioned refusing to sign Rafe Montoya's petition to save the cottage. "I hadn't planned to move right away, but that might be the best thing, to get her settled before she starts high school. At least she won't have to endure any more disruptions."

A weight settled onto Diane's chest. "People in Harmony Circle will accept you, and I think Brea Academy can provide the nurturing she needs. While the kids may be upset about the jury business now, that should blow over quickly."

"I understand, but in the meantime, she's really torn up. The fact that she left her camera bothers me a lot. If she isn't taking photos, what's she doing?"

As they went downstairs, Diane forced herself to concentrate on what mattered most: his daughter's safety. "I could tell she felt bad when my sister shot her mouth off. Then learning that her mother's leaving…" That didn't necessarily indicate immediate danger. *But it'll be dark soon. Where's she gone?*

"I'm going to drive around and look for her." The decision seemed to bolster Josh's spirits.

Diane wanted to help, too. "Brittany and I will go door to door. Someone in the neighborhood might have seen her."

"Thanks." At the bottom of the steps, Josh paused to smooth the hair from Diane's temple. "Having you here means a lot."

Then, don't leave. She longed to hold him tight and feel

the length of his body against hers. But they had more immediate concerns. And her daughter was rounding the corner from the den. "What'd you find?"

Diane told her about the camera and their plans.

"Grandma can phone people in the development. She knows practically everybody."

"Great idea."

They were going to find Carly safe. Diane couldn't imagine any other possibility.

AN HOUR later, Josh had crisscrossed the development repeatedly and driven the surrounding streets without luck. In case Carly had decided to walk east to their old neighborhood in La Habra, a distance of about five miles, he'd driven that route as well and called her friends. No one had seen her.

Diane's canvassing had alerted Rafe Montoya, who'd organized a search party to comb a brushy area north of Harmony Circle. So far, they'd found nothing. Nor had Carly returned to Josh's house, where Diane's mother stood watch.

Josh swung toward his house. This time, he was ready to call the cops.

For good measure, he took one more turn around the horseshoe, braking sharply as, without warning, the Lester boys zoomed off the sidewalk on their skateboards. Stupid kids. Didn't they understand how precious their lives were?

Something about the skateboards nagged at him. As Josh reached home, the significance registered.

Carly's photos. A teenage boy on a skateboard, in this neighborhood. Had they met up tonight? It was a long shot, but he'd try anything.

On his front porch, Lois Oldham stood talking to Rafe. Both regarded him questioningly.

"I haven't found her, but I just remembered something. Please come with me, both of you." He took the stairs at a clip.

In his office, Josh clicked onto Carly's Web site. The blasted thing loaded with agonizing slowness, and at first he feared she might have deleted the pictures. But there they were. "Do either of you recognize this kid?"

"I've seen him around," Lois said.

Rafe did better. "That's Larry Greeves. I've repaired his car. His family lives directly below Minnie."

"His mother must be Annabeth Greeves!" Lois exclaimed. "She used to be my student at Brea Academy."

"Do you have her phone number?" Josh tried not to yield to rising hope. This boy might know nothing about Carly.

"I'm sure I have it at home," Lois said

"Don't bother." Rafe was thumbing through a phone book. "They're listed." He read the number out loud as Josh dialed. When a woman answered, he introduced himself and offered a short explanation.

"I'm sorry." She sounded sympathetic. "My son isn't here."

"Was he in the neighborhood a couple of hours ago?"

"Why, yes."

Progress at last. "Any idea where he went?"

"To a birthday party. A college student who graduated from the high school last year. Larry's a senior," she added.

"Did he take a girl with him?"

"Boys that age, they don't tell their parents much."

Neither do twelve-year-old girls. "May I have his cell number?"

To Josh's relief, she provided it.

Downstairs, more people entered. Diane's voice drifted upward. "Hello? What's going on?"

"I'll tell them." Lois slipped off.

Josh braced for the possibility of a no-service reply. Instead, a young man answered on the fifth ring. "Yeah?" Loud music pounded in the background.

"Larry Greeves?"

"Last time I looked." A smart aleck.

He wasted no time. "I'm trying to find my twelve-year-old daughter, Carly Lorenz. About five-feet-three with long brown hair and braces. Have you seen her?"

In the silence that ensued, he feared they'd lost contact. Then Larry asked nervously, "How old did you say she was?"

"Twelve."

"Oh, my God."

"What did you do?" Josh roared.

"Nothing, man! She said she was sixteen."

"Does she look sixteen to you?" His little girl didn't appear a day over, well, thirteen. Fourteen in a pinch.

"She's around here somewhere. She's been a real pain, asking to go home. I didn't want to miss all the fun. I'll bring her right now."

A seventeen-year-old boy who'd probably been drinking was going to drive Josh's little girl? "Where are you? I'll pick her up."

"I don't know the address."

"Well, find it in a hurry, or I'll bring the police with me."

In short order, Larry reported a location near Cal State Fullerton. "You wait in front with my daughter," Josh instructed.

"No cops, okay?"

"Fine. Just be there. And she'd better be in good shape."

"Yes, sir."

Josh scarcely dared yield to the relief pouring through him. Until he saw Carly, he refused to let down his guard.

On the ground floor, after he explained, Diane said, "Thank heaven. We'd like to come, too, if you don't mind."

"Fine." Josh was grateful for the company. Also, having passengers would remind him not to run red lights or break the speed limit.

He, Diane and Brittany piled into the truck. For several miles, no one spoke. Then the girl asked, "Are you going to punish her?"

"I suspected she's already been punished," Josh answered. "According to Larry, she's been anxious to go home."

"I'd never lie about my age, or go off with a boy and not tell Mom." After a moment, Brittany added, "But I guess she was so upset about other stuff, she couldn't think straight."

"We all make mistakes," Diane noted. "Learning from them is what matters."

"I can vouch for that." Josh swung left onto Imperial Highway, a main thoroughfare.

He appreciated her willingness to hear him out this afternoon. Even if they weren't able to recover the wonderful momentum of this past weekend, he was grateful to be on friendly terms again.

And he hadn't given up aiming for more. Not by a long shot.

Ten minutes later—he'd stayed on the upper edge of the speed limit and skimmed through a few yellow lights—they reached an apartment complex in Fullerton. To Josh's joy, he spotted his daughter, hands thrust in jeans pockets, fidgeting on the sidewalk beside a young man.

He pulled to the curb. A flash of uncertainty crossed her face when he got out.

"It's all right." Josh opened his arms. "I'm not mad."

She launched herself at him. Finally Josh accepted, deep down, that everything was going to be all right.

Chapter Sixteen

A bittersweet mixture of joy and longing filled Diane at the sight of Josh hugging his daughter with such fierce protectiveness. These two shared a special bond, just as she and Brittany did.

Thank heaven Carly was out of harm's way. Yet the recovery freed Diane's mind to flash back to that computer screen filled with real estate listings.

All along, beneath the surface, she'd sensed an intangible quality that might pull Josh away. She hadn't even consciously recognized it, but she did now. The sense of belonging, the bonds that meant so much to her threatened him. He longed for isolation, for distance.

From Harmony Circle or from me, too?

Freed of his responsibility, Larry Greeves loped back into the complex. With luck, he'd take more care with young girls after this. Perhaps he'd truly believed Carly was sixteen, but most likely, he hadn't cared...until her father showed up.

Family ties protected kids. Best of all was to have a couple of loving parents. Despite the good fortune of having a grandmother and aunt across the street, Brittany needed a dad, too.

She'd begun to hope, this weekend, that that might be Josh. But she'd better not count on it.

He opened the passenger door for his daughter. She glanced at the passengers in surprise. "You guys came, too?"

"The whole neighborhood's been looking for you," Brit burst out.

Carly fastened her seat belt. "I'm sorry. When Larry invited me to a birthday party, I figured we'd eat cake and be back in an hour."

"You should have borrowed a phone and called me." The lights of oncoming traffic silhouetted Josh's head and shoulders as he started the truck.

"I was afraid you'd get mad," his daughter admitted. "I thought about walking home, but it's too far."

"I'm glad you didn't try that. Staying put was a wise choice." Tenderness shone in his eyes as he glanced at her.

"Did people really search for me?"

"It was cool!" Brit launched into an account of the door-to-door expedition. Diane contributed details, and Josh threw in an anecdote from his own search.

His headlights had confused a cat on the verge of a pounce, allowing a chipmunk to escape. "Judging by the disgust on that cat's face, I'd have been in big trouble if I were a little smaller."

They chuckled at the thought. A few hours earlier, they'd been returning from their trip under tense circumstances, Diane recalled. Who'd have thought another crisis would bring them together again? For a little while, anyway.

A group lingered outside number 18. The cheer that arose brought a disbelieving grin to Carly's face. "Wow! Is that for me?"

"Who else?" Josh teased.

Brittany pumped a fist in a victory salute. "You're a celebrity."

Suzy ran over. "Don't you ever do that again," she scolded her friend. "I was worried sick."

"I'm sorry." Carly hopped down. Diane was delighted when Brittany joined them for a group hug.

"We bought you a camouflage apron in Oceanside," Carly announced.

"Can I see it?"

"Sure. It's on my bed."

"We're going to wear them as a sort of uniform," Brittany told her.

After a quick thank-you to the onlookers, the three friends hurried into the house. Rafe shook Josh's hand. "I'm glad you found her."

"Me, too. I appreciate your help. And everyone's."

Amid the chorus of congratulations, Sarah hung back. If she dared mention the trial again, Diane might have to bestow a big-sisterly rebuke. Or possibly a chokehold.

Finally most of the others left, and Sarah approached Josh. "I'm sorry about making a scene earlier. I didn't consider how my outburst might affect your daughter."

"You aren't to blame for her disappearing," he answered.

"Nevertheless, I went off half-cocked." Sarah cast an apologetic glance at Diane. "I've been talking to Mom about what it's like to serve on a jury. And about, well, blaming you for what Hector Fry did, when it's not your fault."

"Believe me, I wish I could go back and change my vote," Josh assured her.

"If you're willing, I'd like to put the whole business behind us," Sarah said.

"That suits me."

The two shook hands, after which Diane gave her sister a hug. They clung to each other for a long moment.

When they separated, Diane felt relieved—and exhausted. It had been a long day. As soon as her sister left, she said goodbye to Josh, collected Brittany and headed down the slope.

Her daughter lingered in the den. "Mom?"

"What, honey?"

The girl hesitated. "I... Oh, it doesn't matter."

Her ragged tone clued Diane that this might be important. "Tell me."

"Promise you won't get mad," Brittany said.

"Of course not." What *was* this?

A deep breath. "When Josh hugged Carly, in front of the apartments, I envied her a little. For having a dad, I guess. I wished he cared that much about me, too." The girl blinked away a tear. "Was that wrong?"

"Not at all." *I felt the same way.* "Every girl needs a father, and he's a terrific one."

"You don't think Dad would mind?"

Diane's gaze flew to the photos on the wall. Will bathed them in his warm gaze. "He'd choose the same thing I would, for you to be surrounded by people who cherish you. Nobody can replace Dad. That doesn't mean we can't find room in our hearts for someone else in the future."

"I was hoping you'd say that." Having received validation, Brittany went upstairs humming.

Diane resumed studying the images of Will. She especially loved one that showed his glasses sliding down his nose. It showed his funny, endearing side.

They'd grown up together. Shared the experience of launching their teaching careers and the miracle of creating a child. He'd been her dearest friend.

She regarded their wedding photo, Will in his tuxedo, her in a lace gown. On that special day, they'd promised to stay together as long as they both should live. And so they had.

With a jolt, Diane realized she was saying goodbye. Not to Will's memory, which would stay with her forever. But to the sense, deep in her soul, that they were still married.

In the intervening years, she'd grown through tragedy and learned to cope without him. Now, in a new relationship, she'd reached a turning point.

The prospect of change scared the heck out of her. But although Josh hadn't asked anything of her, Diane might have to make a difficult choice in order to keep him.

She suspected Will would have urged her to take the chance.

IF JOSH had imagined his troubles were over, he'd been mistaken.

On Tuesday, the police captured a second gang member suspected in the shooting, and the clerk left the hospital. Good news, but the paper also ran a statement from the jury foreman that Hector's guilt had been obvious to everyone "except that knucklehead Lorenz."

Ouch.

Later in the day, he found a flier in his mailbox from the homeowners' association. A special meeting was scheduled for the next weekend to discuss whether the community should hire a lawyer to fight for cottage preservation.

He nearly groaned aloud. Couldn't he just, for once, fit in with everyone else? But much as he'd appreciated the neighbors' help in finding his daughter, he didn't feel as if he fitted into Harmony Circle. Too much of a loner, he supposed.

On the plus side, Carly returned from school pleased that the principal had decided to organize a photography club and appoint her as student adviser. "I promised not to misuse my camera again. I have to set an example for the younger kids."

Dr. Kenton might have concocted this idea on her own, but Josh suspected he owed equal gratitude to Diane. As a thank-you gift, he decided to till her garden next spring.

If he was still here.

He missed their easy comradeship of the previous weekend. He dreamed about her and longed to be alone with her again. He'd call her soon, he resolved.

The following day, near five o'clock, Josh lingered in his office, reviewing the specs for a remodeling job. The rumble of a heavy truck on Lambert Road reverberated through the one-story building, which sat in the middle of a gravel yard. At this hour, the secretary had already left, along with everyone else. Construction crews started and ended their days early to reduce travel time on busy freeways.

Restlessly, Josh checked a subcontractor's bid. The figure for tile work looked low. He'd better make sure the man planned to use top-quality materials.

From the outer office, light footsteps tapped the floor. A prospective client? A tradesman?

Dropping the specs on his cluttered desk, Josh finger-combed his springy hair. Darn. He'd probably smudged his face and his clothes weren't exactly pristine. Despite regular cleaning, piles of dust drifted into the building.

"Hello? Josh?" called a woman's voice.

The familiar tone sent him hurrying to the outer office, smudge or no smudge. What a pleasant surprise. Diane looked even more radiant than usual, her fresh skin and sunny yellow dress glowing in contrast to the drab cabinets and faded blueprints on the walls.

"Hi. Sorry the place is such a mess." Josh wished someone

had removed the empty coffee cup from the windowsill and wiped a workman's dirty shoeprints from the linoleum.

"Oliver said you'd probably be alone at this hour." She eased close enough for him to smell flowers and fresh soap. "I hope it's okay to drop by unannounced."

"It's fine." He'd have offered her a seat, but he didn't trust any of the chairs not to ruin her pretty dress.

"We need to talk." She hovered uncertainly across the room. "I purposely chose your territory. I thought you'd feel more comfortable here."

That made no sense to Josh. "We should have met at a restaurant so you wouldn't need a bath afterward."

"Don't apologize." Diane gestured around her. "I like this place. It's unpretentious and functional, like a classroom."

"Yeah, it's the height of something or other."

She folded her arms. "Don't be sarcastic, or I'll lose track of what I came to say."

A sudden twist of the gut warned that perhaps she'd come to break off with him. "Is this bad news, like you're building a spite fence between our properties? Maybe I should hurry up and move."

"No. Because when you do, I'm willing to go with you."

Dust must be clogging Josh's airways, because suddenly he had trouble breathing. "What?"

"That didn't sound right. It was presumptuous."

He couldn't have understood her correctly. "I'm not sure I follow you. Or any of this."

"I'll try to put it in perspective." Diane fidgeted with her purse strap. "Like kids, adults go through stages, only we don't realize we're in one until we've outgrown it."

"I'm sorry?" What did this have to do with her declaration about going with him?

"Bear with me, okay?"

"Sure." The recognition that this usually articulate woman was struggling for words touched Josh.

"We have to accept who we are, not who we used to be. I grew up in Harmony Circle—it's my comfort zone. But people are more important than places."

He must be dense, because he still didn't grasp the point. "It's the people who count. That's why living near your family and friends matters so much to you," he interpreted.

"No. If things work out between us…" She hesitated.

If things work out. Was that still possible?

Josh hadn't dared consider a long-term future with Diane. He'd never really felt he belonged anywhere and, whenever he'd tried to get close to anyone other than his daughter, he'd made a mess of it. He'd taken refuge in distances, emotional and physical.

Losing Tiffany had hurt, but she'd never become a part of him the way Diane had, even in this short time. Without meaning to, he'd opened his heart. Was it possible she'd done the same?

He hardly dared breathe.

She pressed on. "I'm wondering if…if someday there might be room on that dream property of yours for Brittany and me. I mean, I wanted to let you know that I'm willing to consider it. To consider moving. That I'm not tied to one place."

A part of him longed to shout his delight. And yet, that imaginary sanctuary had become his buffer, a guarantee that he had a place to retreat if the rest of his world collapsed.

He couldn't imagine that Diane would really give up so much for him. Or that she wouldn't quickly tire of living in an isolated place with him.

As the silence stretched, he saw doubt creep into her expression. She closed her eyes, and when they reopened, tears sparkled. "Josh, I apologize. I've put you in an awkward position."

Say something. If he did, though, it might be the wrong thing.

She turned, as if unwilling to stay another second. "Let's forget we had this conversation, all right?"

He didn't want to forget it. When had he become a coward, anyway? Let the woman shatter his heart. Maybe that wouldn't happen for months or years, and in the meantime, he might discover what happiness felt like.

"I love you," Josh said.

She halted, facing the other way.

He closed the distance between them in a couple of strides. To hell with smudging her dress. He caught the woman he loved and spun her around.

She was crying. Oh, damn. He hadn't expected that. "I hope those are the joyful kind of tears."

Diane nodded and then flung her arms around his neck. "I love you, too, you idiot."

Against his chest, she felt warm and intensely alive. "You think I'm an idiot?" he murmured.

"You nearly let me walk out of here."

"I'm slow on the uptake." Josh stopped talking to kiss her. That felt so good, he kissed her again.

When they finally eased apart, Diane said, "In case you were worried, I'm not asking for promises."

He didn't trust promises, anyway. "I'm *not* worried. You hungry?"

"Starving."

"Your place or mine?"

"Both," she said. "How about if you grill hamburgers and

I fix a salad? Brittany went home with a friend, but I promised to pick her up before dinner."

"You're on." Josh beamed down at her. "Guess I'm going to have to build you a gazebo after all. So we can meet in the middle."

"I'd say we're already pretty good at that."

They went outside together, holding hands.

Chapter Seventeen

The next six weeks flew by, packed with so many memorable experiences that Diane could barely keep track of them.

She supposed everyone must notice the energy with which she greeted each day. Josh's kindness and strength surrounded her even when they were apart.

At school, she loved watching his daughter blossom as she mentored less-experienced photographers. In addition, several evenings a week, the two small families gathered to discuss the days' events over meals.

For Halloween, she and Josh took the girls to a party at Diane's church. Brittany served the younger children home-baked treats, while Carly took pictures of them in costume.

Three minor issues disturbed Diane's contentment. The first was that she and Josh didn't have enough time alone. While they managed the occasional afternoon or evening without the girls, she longed to sleep in his arms again.

Second, he was going about transforming his house with single-minded purpose. The hammering and the sounds of equipment served as a reminder to her of his zeal to finish. To be gone from Harmony Circle. Despite her decision that their relationship came first, she shrank from the prospect of leaving this place she loved.

Third, Josh had mentioned nothing further about acquiring a larger property, nor did he offer a tour of the remodeling efforts. Why was he keeping her at arm's length? Had he spoken in haste that afternoon at his office, and did he regret it?

He'd said he loved her, and he'd repeated it several times since. Nothing in his treatment of her indicated otherwise. So she trusted him and tried not to worry.

On Thanksgiving Day, when Lois, Sarah and Diane hosted a gathering at number 2 Harmony Road, he greeted everyone by name. Yet he stood a little apart, as if ill at ease in company.

Among the guests were Alice and George. For them, too, the past few months had wrought significant changes.

Following their square-dancing date, they'd talk for hours, which Alice had recounted at a meeting of the Foxes. George had explained that, fifty years ago, he'd been leery about the strength he sensed in Alice. He hadn't had the self-confidence—or modern consciousness—to appreciate her forthright nature.

Instead, he'd married Lise, a traditional, compliant wife. She'd stayed home to tend their two children, staying in the background until their son had died in a motorcycle crash.

George had suffered a severe depression, he'd confessed. Lise insisted on psychiatric treatment, and she'd taken a job as a saleswoman until he recovered.

He'd realized then the value of an equal partner, and they'd enjoyed a rewarding relationship until her death. In his mature years, he felt ready to rediscover the qualities that had attracted him to Alice in the first place.

They'd been dating ever since. Diane had never seen her former principal in such high spirits.

Among the other guests, Oliver and Renée maintained an easy camaraderie. While setting the dining table alongside

Diane, the hairdresser chose that private moment to say, "Isn't he fun? It's great to find a guy who doesn't try to put a ball and chain on me."

Diane handed her a batch of silverware. "Marriage doesn't interest you?"

Renée gave a delicate shudder. "Being single suits me fine."

To each her own. Personally, Diane valued connections above independence. As for Josh, she hoped he'd grown to share that sentiment.

A short time later, as the group formed a circle to offer a prayer of thanks, her heart swelled with gratitude. For Josh's solid presence beside her, for the two girls bowing their heads side by side, for her mother and sister, and for old friends.

Afterward, the girls handled cleanup while the adults gathered in the den to watch a football game on TV. Josh pulled Diane aside. "I'd like to stretch my legs. This might be a good chance to show you the remodeling, if you're in the mood. It's nearly done."

Excitement flared. Finally, he was allowing her inside his project. "I'd love to see it."

"Don't mention the house to the others. They might try to tag along and I could use a breather."

"Agreed." Being alone with him was exactly what Diane had hoped for.

Then his words sank in. *Nearly done.* Did that mean he—they?—would be leaving soon?

She took a quiet leave of her mother and threw on a sweater. Out they went into the brisk afternoon, strolling around the U-shape of Harmony Road. Rafe's house was dark—he'd planned to drive his niece and nephew to visit their grandparents in Los Angeles, he'd explained in declining Lois's invitation.

Diane wished she'd be here to watch those kids grow up. At most, she'd catch glimpses when she visited Lois and Sarah.

In front of the empty cottage, a Sold banner half-covered the For Sale sign. Were Sherry and Winston really going to tear down that adorable cottage? Would they ever make peace with their neighbors?

Diane reassured herself that she'd find out. For heaven's sake, she planned to rent her house, not sell it, so she would remain a homeowner.

If only Josh would slow down and put his arm around her, she might feel more relaxed. Instead, he had to keep checking his stride to let her catch up. What was his hurry?

At last they reached number 18. From the walkway, Diane admired the new door with its sunburst pattern of glass panes. Inside, they encountered the smells of sawdust and paint.

The living room came alive with fresh color. Proudly, Josh shepherded her into the kitchen. At last he spoke freely— about the details of cabinetry, the pullout shelves and the efficiently designed pantry.

Impressed, Diane took in the double ovens and cooking island, the oak cabinets and granite counters. "Brittany would adore this."

"How about you?" He quirked an eyebrow.

"It's fabulous."

"Wait'll you see the rest."

They went on to inspect the freshly carpeted dining room and the full bath that replaced the old downstairs powder room. Diane envied the future owners, whoever they might be. "You thought of everything."

"I enjoyed the challenge."

She wandered through the house with him, admiring the

craftsmanship and attention to detail. Josh had lavished this place with as much care as if he planned to occupy it himself.

He made no attempt to take advantage of their privacy, to hold her or kiss her. Diane wondered if he valued her half as much as he valued his handiwork.

Upstairs, the bathroom shone with new amenities, but he hadn't quite finished the master suite. In the clear light pouring through curtainless windows, Josh held up a book of fabric samples. "Do any of these curtain fabrics appeal to you, or would you prefer miniblinds?"

Diane fingered a flower pattern in southwestern colors. "This is gorgeous, but shouldn't you leave that decision to the buyers?"

"Buyers." He snapped his fingers. "I knew there was something I forgot."

She tensed. "You found someone already?"

Josh set down the samples. "Not exactly. The past six weeks, well, doesn't our arrangement seem a little unsatisfying to you?"

Unsatisfying. The word sent a tremor of worry through Diane. *He's got a talent for pushing people away,* Renée had warned.

Perhaps he'd changed his mind about wanting her to go with him. "You feel trapped?"

"Frustrated would be more accurate." Josh shifted closer. How dear every detail had become—the smile lines around his eyes, the quizzical curve of his mouth. "I'm impatient with juggling schedules to steal a few hours alone."

"So am I." If Diane was reading him correctly, he *did* plan for them to live together, and sooner than she'd anticipated. The prospect both thrilled and saddened her. "I guess you're anxious to get settled in your new—our new—place."

"Aren't you?"

"What?"

"Eager to move?"

"Well…" In all honesty, she wished she could have him *and* her community. That hardly seemed romantic, though. "I choose to be with you, Josh."

He closed the book of fabric samples. "The thing is, I'm not as keen on living in the middle of nowhere as I used to be. When I was a kid, crammed into apartments with my folks, I used to dream about open space. Being around you, I've discovered I like the space I'm in."

"You mean Harmony Circle?" Diane scarcely dared believe it. "You want to stay in this neighborhood?"

"That's about the size of it."

"You're sure you can tolerate neighbors who poke their noses into our business?"

"If they do that too much, I may tell them to butt out," Josh admitted. "But the better I know them, the more I appreciate how much they care about each other. I'm fixing this house up to live in, not to sell. Now, what do you think about the curtains?"

Despite her relief, Diane felt a twinge of disappointment. If they were staying, they wouldn't be moving in together any time soon. "You should pick whatever suits you."

He blinked. "Me?"

"You're the one who lives here."

Josh shook his head. "What I'm trying to suggest, in my inept manner, is that we should both wake up in this room every morning, eat breakfast in that state-of-the-art kitchen and brush our teeth in those twin sinks. I've been selfish enough to pick most of the decor myself, but that was before, well, before I got my act together."

She longed to agree, but how would they handle the gossip? If they lived far away, that might not affect them, but this situation would prove awkward in a lot of ways.

"We have to consider how this will affect the girls," she

told him ruefully. "And my mom and Sarah. Call me old-fashioned…"

He caught her hands. "Wait!"

"Wait for what?"

He glanced at the floor, a welter of rough boards awaiting carpet. "Is it okay if I don't do the kneeling thing?"

The kneeling thing. "It's not necessary," she mumbled, afraid to trust the spurt of joy his words inspired.

"Good. Diane Bittner, will you marry me?"

If only she could capture this moment and savor it forever, like a scene in a glass globe. *Like one of Carly's photographs, except I'm living inside it.*

"You do want to marry me, don't you?" Eagerness and uncertainty trembled in his voice. "You mean more to me than anything, Diane."

The love she'd never expected to find again filled her heart. "Oh, yes. Of course I'll marry you, Josh!"

"Yes!" he shouted, and took her in his arms. They clung together, laughing and kissing. She'd have stayed there forever if that were possible.

The next best thing was to make plans and turn this fantasy into reality. "We could get married in the spring."

"Do we have to wait that long?"

"Weddings involve a lot of planning."

"I'm sorry for rushing you." Josh paused for all of five seconds before adding, "But sooner is better."

Quit trying to control everything and let this happen.

"I've had my big white frilly ceremony," Diane conceded. "How about a Christmas wedding? Then we can celebrate the holidays in our new home."

"*That* I like."

They went downstairs and snuggled on the couch, discussing all sorts of things. The ceremony. What role the girls would play. How to combine their households.

Above all, how very, very happy they were

At last they returned to her mother's house and took their daughters aside. The gleeful screams of "We're going to be sisters!" spoiled the surprise for everyone else, but no one minded.

Not at all.

CHRISTMAS and New Year's flew by. Diane was so busy she scarcely had time to breathe.

In mid-January, she finally finished arranging the new display in the den and stood back to admire it. Outside, she could hear Josh and the girls laughing as they played badminton in the yard.

In a center spot, she'd hung a formal portrait of the wedding party on the church steps. Diane wore a champagne-hued suit, Josh was in a tux and the two girls were giggling in maroon dresses. His parents looked healthy and happy, up on a visit from Guatemala, and her mother was radiant in Christmas green. Only the expressions of best man Oliver Armstrong and maid of honor Sarah Oldham had stiffened from smiling too much, but they'd been as merry as everyone else at the reception.

In truth, though, Diane preferred Carly's candid shots. One, labeled The Creation of the Wedding Cake, showed a dab of frosting on Brittany's nose and a splash of flour bedecking Lois's apron. Forgiveness captured Sarah giving her brother-in-law an impromptu hug.

In a special kids' corner, Diane had placed the girls' nostalgic favorites: baby Brittany in Will's arms and a beribboned toddler Carly held by Tiffany. In a group shot, the newly formed Brea Academy Photography Club gathered around Carly, its president.

There was room for more images to come, as well. Including, no doubt, a shot Carly would snap when she visited her new half-brother in New York during spring break. And perhaps someday another baby in this home, too. Diane, of all people, knew that, when one circle of life closes, another has a way of opening.

As time went by, she mused, there'd be plenty of memories created at number 18, Harmony Road. Right now, though, she and Josh were so busy enjoying each tumultuous day and long, uninterrupted night that she rarely had a chance to think about such things.

With one last, fond glance at the wall of memories, Diane went outside to join her family.

* * * * *

Find out more about what's happening
in Harmony Circle with
Jacqueline Diamond's next book in the series,
BABY IN WAITING,
coming August 2008 only from
Harlequin American Romance.

THOROUGHBRED LEGACY
The stakes are high when it comes to love,
horse racing, family secrets
and broken promises.

A new exciting Harlequin continuity series coming soon!
Led by New York Times *bestselling author*
Elizabeth Bevarly
FLIRTING WITH TROUBLE

Here's a preview!

THE DOOR CLOSED behind them, throwing them into darkness and leaving them utterly alone. And the next thing Daniel knew, he heard himself saying, "Marnie, I'm sorry about the way things turned out in Del Mar."

She said nothing at first, only strode across the room and stared out the window beside him. Although he couldn't see her well in the darkness—he still hadn't switched on a light… but then, neither had she—he imagined her expression was a little preoccupied, a little anxious, a little confused.

Finally, very softly, she said, "Are you?"

He nodded, then, worried she wouldn't be able to see the gesture, added, "Yeah. I am. I should have said goodbye to you."

"Yes, you should have."

Actually, he thought, there were a lot of things he should have done in Del Mar. He'd had *a lot* riding on the Pacific Classic, and even more on his entry, Little Joe, but after meeting Marnie, the Pacific Classic had been the last thing on Daniel's mind. His loss at Del Mar had pretty much ended his career before it had even begun, and he'd had to start all over again, rebuilding from nothing.

He simply had not then and did not now have room in his life for a woman as potent as Marnie Roberts. He was a horseman first and foremost. From the time he was a schoolboy, he'd known what he wanted to do with his life—be the best possible trainer he could be.

He had to make sure Marnie understood—and he understood, too—why things had ended the way they had eight years ago. He just wished he could find the words to do that. Hell, he wished he could find the *thoughts* to do that.

"You made me forget things, Marnie, things that I really needed to remember. And that scared the hell out of me. Little Joe should have won the Classic. He was by far the best horse entered in that race. But I didn't give him the attention he needed and deserved that week, because all I could think about was you. Hell, when I woke up that morning all I wanted to do was lie there and look at you, and then wake you up and make love to you again. If I hadn't left when I did— the way I did—I might still be lying there in that bed with you, thinking about nothing else."

"And would that be so terrible?" she asked.

"Of course not," he told her. "But that wasn't why I was in Del Mar," he repeated. "I was in Del Mar to win a race. That was my job. And my work was the most important thing to me."

She said nothing for a moment, only studied his face in the darkness as if looking for the answer to a very important question. Finally she asked, "And what's the most important thing to you now, Daniel?"

Wasn't the answer to that obvious? "My work," he answered automatically.

She nodded slowly. "Of course," she said softly. "That is, after all, what you do best."

Her comment, too, puzzled him. She made it sound as if being good at what he did was a bad thing.

She bit her lip thoughtfully, her eyes fixed on his, glimmering in the scant moonlight that was filtering through the window. And damned if Daniel didn't find himself wanting to pull her into his arms and kiss her. But as much as it might have felt as if no time had passed since Del Mar, there were eight years between now and then. And eight years was a long time in the best of circumstances. For Daniel and Marnie, it was virtually a lifetime.

So Daniel turned and started for the door, then halted. He couldn't just walk away and leave things as they were, unsettled. He'd done that eight years ago and regretted it.

"It *was* good to see you again, Marnie," he said softly. And since he was being honest, he added, "I hope we see each other again."

She didn't say anything in response, only stood silhouetted against the window with her arms wrapped around her in a way that made him wonder whether she was doing it because she was cold, or if she just needed something—someone— to hold on to. In either case, Daniel understood. There was an emptiness clinging to him that he suspected would be there for a long time.

* * * * *

THOROUGHBRED LEGACY
coming soon wherever books are sold!

Thoroughbred *Legacy*

Launching in June 2008

A dramatic new 12-book continuity that embodies the American Dream.

Meet the Prestons, owners of Quest Stables, a successful horse-racing and breeding empire. But the lives, loves and reputations of this hardworking family are put at risk when a breeding scandal unfolds.

Flirting with Trouble

by *New York Times* bestselling author

ELIZABETH BEVARLY

Eight years ago, publicist Marnie Roberts spent seven days of bliss with Australian horse trainer Daniel Whittleson. But just as quickly, he disappeared. Now Marnie is heading to Australia to finally confront the man she's never been able to forget.

The stakes are high when it comes to love, horse racing, family secrets and broken promises.

A new exciting Harlequin continuity series coming soon!

Cole's Red-Hot Pursuit

Cole Westmoreland is a man who gets what he
wants. And he wants independent and sultry
Patrina Forman! She resists him—until a Montana
blizzard traps them together. For three delicious
nights, Cole indulges Patrina with his brand of
seduction. When the sun comes out, Cole and
Patrina are left to wonder—will this be the end of
the passion that storms between them?

Look for

COLE'S RED-HOT
PURSUIT

by USA TODAY bestselling author

BRENDA
JACKSON

Available in June 2008 wherever you buy books.

Always Powerful, Passionate and Provocative.

REQUEST YOUR FREE BOOKS!

2 FREE NOVELS PLUS 2
FREE GIFTS!

Heart, Home & Happiness!

HAR08

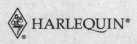
HARLEQUIN®

American ★ Romance®

COMING NEXT MONTH

#1213 TEXAS LULLABY by Tina Leonard
The State of Parenthood
Gabriel Morgan has been lured home to Union Junction, Texas, by a father who
claims his intentions have nothing to do with matching his ornery son with a
ready-made family. Gabriel has his commitment radar up—so when he lays eyes
on Laura Adams and her sweet children, he's not prepared for the visions of
baby booties dancing in his head!

#1214 MAN OF THE YEAR by Lisa Ruff
From their first meeting, sparks fly between Samantha James and Jarrett Corliss.
But Samantha wants nothing to do with the arrogant baseball player. Besides, the
team's owner has decreed that there will be no hint of scandal or heads will roll.
Jarrett sees Samantha's aloofness as a challenge, and he's not going to let her get
away, whatever the boss says.

#1215 AN HONORABLE TEXAN by Victoria Chancellor
Brody's Crossing
Eighteen months ago Cal Crawford left his Texas ranch for deployment overseas,
and has returned to find out he's a father. The traditional Cal wants to marry
the mother, but Christie Simmons needs to know they are together for love, and
not just for the sake of the baby. Can their weekend tryst turn into a lifetime of
happiness?

#1216 RELUCTANT PARTNERS by Kara Lennox
Second Sons
When Cooper Remington arrives in Port Clara, Texas, to collect his inheritance,
he finds a surprise—an entrancing redhead, claiming Uncle Johnny left his boat
to her! Cooper is sure Allie Bateman is a gold digger—and he will do whatever
is necessary to win what is rightfully his.

www.eHarlequin.com

HARCNM0508